HOMETOWN GAL

A Wine Flights of Murder Series Prequel

Paul Skalny

Skalmystoricpoe, LLC | SHELBY TOWNSHIP | MICHIGAN

Copyright © 2024 Paul Skalny

All rights reserved

The characters and events portrayed in this book are fictitious. Any similarity to real persons, living or dead, is coincidental and not intended by the author.

No part of this book may be reproduced, or stored in a retrieval system, or transmitted in any form or by any means, electronic, mechanical, photocopying, recording, or otherwise, without express written permission of the publisher.

ISBN-13: 9798333065810 (Paperback)
ISBN-13: 9798333076151 (Hardcover)

Published by Skalmystoricpoe, LLC
Shelby Township, Michigan

skalmystoricpoe.com

Cover Photograph by: Paul Skalny
Library of Congress Control Number: 2024915329
Printed in the United States of America

To my mom, Sophie, who waited for my dad, Staff Sergeant John F. Skalny, a waist gunner aboard a B-17 bomber, to return safely home in 1945. Thankfully, they married not long after his return; otherwise, I wouldn't be here.

Dear Reader,

Thank you for purchasing this prequel in the *Wine Flights of Murder* series.

Hometown Gal is published by Skalmystoricpoe, LLC, a small independent publisher.

Please consider leaving a review or rating at the site of your purchase. Reviews help us to reach a greater audience and are always appreciated.

The *Wine Flights of Murder* series also includes the already published, *Russian Red*. In 2025, another prequel and a sequel are expected to be published.

Other books published by Skalmystoricpoe, LLC, include *Best Friends, Best Forgotten* and *Best Friends, Best Forgiven*, the first two novels in the *Best Friends, Best Forgotten* series.

Visit **wineflightsofmurder.com** for the latest information on the *Wine Flights of Murder* series.

See the Proof-of-Concept Movie Trailer for *Best Friends, Best Forgotten* and learn how you can help make the full-length feature film a reality at **BFBFMovie.com**.

CHAPTER 1

Dusk set over the Russian River Valley after another day of glorious sunshine. The golden light faded, giving way to a gentle twilight that cast a soft, purplish hue over the vineyards and homes dotted across the Valley's landscape. The faint scent of ripening grapes and the hum of hummingbirds taking their last sips from the feeders filled the air. The soothing sounds of crickets began their evening chorus, adding a harmonious backdrop to the tranquil scene.

Blondie and Gunner sat back on the west side of their wraparound porch and admired the scene gracing many of their late summer evenings. The wooden boards of the porch were warm under their feet, still holding the sun's heat. Quiet ruled the moment until Gunner spoke, his voice breaking the serene spell.

"I'll never grow tired of the beauty that lies each early evening at our doorstep," he said, his gaze fixed on the horizon where the last light lingered.

Blondie turned to him with a soft smile, her eyes reflecting the twilight's glow. "It's our little slice of paradise," she replied, her voice barely above a whisper, as if not to disturb the peace surrounding them.

But despite the beauty, a flicker of unease stirred in Gunner's mind, a nagging feeling he couldn't shake. He dismissed it, attributing it to the fatigue of the day.

They had no idea that within a few minutes, the piercing

sound of a police siren winding down Creekside Road would shatter their slice of paradise, stopping right at the base of their long and winding driveway. Perplexed, Gunner rushed to the front side of the porch, but by the time he arrived, no police car was in sight. Blondie followed him gingerly, her gait compromised by the sprained ankle she suffered yesterday morning.

"What's going on?" she asked, her voice laced with concern.

"Nothing. No police car in sight. It's strange," Gunner replied, scanning the area with a puzzled expression.

While Gunner remained standing and puzzled, Blondie, now chilled, decided to go inside, beckoning Gunner to do so as well.

Meanwhile, as dusk turned to evening, two figures dressed in black approached the house silently from the trees surrounding the property's north side. Their faces were hidden, and their night vision goggles illuminated the pitch-dark night. Each appeared to have a weapon in their grasp. Slowly, they made their way toward the house, removing the goggles when the light from within the house started to compromise their night vision.

Gunner and Blondie, now warm on the outside from the heat of the family room's fireplace and warm on the inside from the cups of hot chocolate, sat across from each other at the small table in their kitchen, conversing without knowing that this would be their last intimate conversation. Suddenly, both the back door to the family room and the front door to the house burst open, each masked figure intently focused on subduing the elderly couple.

In a flash, Gunner and Blondie were tied to their chairs, their mouths covered with duct tape. Fear shone in their eyes as one intruder stood guard, watching them intently while the other rummaged through the house. The sound of opening drawers and items being tossed echoed through the rooms. The second intruder finally stopped in the living room, pausing to admire a painting that covered a good portion of the wall behind the long couch.

Blondie and Gunner could only see the second intruder staring at the wall from their vantage point. Each instinctively knew that the intruder was looking at Gunner's painting of their vineyard, affectionately known as "Blondie's." The vineyard sprawled southward for eight acres directly from their house, a cherished symbol of their shared life and labor.

"This is it!" In a moment, after shouting the first words heard by the increasingly agitated couple, the intruder removed the painting. He delicately sliced the paper covering the backside, revealing a small envelope attached to the canvas. Without hesitation, he ripped open the envelope, extracting a handwritten letter dated January 5, 1946. He quickly read it, then walked into the kitchen, his eyes keenly focused on Gunner.

Pushing aside the table, he now moved unimpeded closer to Gunner, his once menacing eyes slowly abating, his gun holstered by his side and the letter in his hand. He held the letter to Gunner's face and ripped off the duct tape covering his mouth.

"What does this mean, old man?"

"Nothing."

"I'll ask you again. What does this letter mean?"

"Like I said before, nothing!"

Looking first at a trembling Blondie and then at Gunner, the masked man in black slowly and angrily shouted, "What does this letter mean?"

"Nothing," Gunner restated. "It's just a good luck charm that I place in every painting I create. It's a copy of the last letter written by Colonel Harrington, my commanding officer in Foggia, Italy, during World War II. He was fond of wine, loved the vineyards in Foggia, and our crew always believed he was our good luck charm."

"You expect me to believe that? A little friendly persuasion for your wife will get you to tell the truth."

Turning away from Gunner, he peered directly into Blondie's eyes, picked up his gun, and pointed it at Blondie's temple. Then he swatted the butt end of the gun against her forehead. Blood flowed easily from the tiny cut.

"Now, will you tell me the truth!"

"I am! I swear," Gunner exclaimed.

"Liar! It's obvious that you're hiding something."

"No, I'm not. Reread the letter. It's just a simple hello and how-are-you-doing letter the Colonel sent me and all the crew members I flew with. Nothing more, nothing less."

"Prove it, or your wife dies!"

"How can I prove it? There are no other paintings of mine in the house. If there were, you would see that each would have the same letter."

Again, Blondie caught the intruder's attention, and he aggressively ripped off the duct tape from her mouth.

"What do you want from us?" Blondie demanded, her voice steady despite her fear. "Just take whatever you want and leave us be."

"We'll leave when we have answers. Tell your husband to cooperate."

"He is. Each of his paintings has a copy of the letter attached to the back of the canvas. I know because I've seen him do so, and I've also been part of some of the conversations he and Colonel Harrington had during the crew's latter reunions."

The intruder turned to Gunner and swatted the butt end of his gun against Gunner's forehead with much more force than he'd used on Blondie.

"Please," Blondie whispered, her voice trembling. "We've

done nothing to deserve this. Get out of here!"

Blondie's eyes focused on Gunner and then darted at both intruders, searching for any sign of hope. She struggled to get free, but the ropes around her wrists held firm. Despite the blow to his head and the dire situation, Gunner maintained a composed expression, all the while trying to free himself from his bonds.

The room fell silent as the tension thickened with each passing second. Blondie's mind raced, recalling the moments that led to this nightmare. They had been enjoying a quiet evening, reminiscing and planning for the future, when the doors burst open, and the intruders shattered their peace.

Without warning, the intruder's sharp voice cut through the silence. "Enough!"

Blondie flinched, tears flowing freely. Gunner clenched his fists, his knuckles white against the coarse ropes, his wrists turning red. Blondie sensed a cold and unforgiving sound in his voice.

"This is not about you or your husband," he said, low and menacing. "This is about something much bigger and important."

Blondie and Gunner exchanged a glance, a silent communication passing between them. They had faced many hardships together, but this felt different—sinister.

"Whatever it is you think we know, we don't," Gunner said, his voice firm. "We're just simple folk. It's just a simple letter. It has no meaning other than being a good luck charm."

He laughed, a hollow, chilling sound. "Simple? Hardly. Whether you realize it or not, you've been part of something complex for a long time."

Blondie's mind spun, trying to piece together the puzzle. What could they possibly be involved in that warranted such violence? Was it something Gunner was involved in that he never confided to her?

"Please, just tell us what you want," she begged. "We can't help you if we don't know what you want."

The intruder moved away, and for a moment, there was a ray of hope until Blondie and Gunner heard, "There's no helping either one of you now."

Blondie's heart sank. She could see the determination in their intruders' eyes, the unwavering resolve to execute whatever sinister plan they had.

Gunner's voice softened, filled with an unspoken apology. "Blondie, I'm so sorry." A tear strolled down his cheek.

Blondie shook her head, tears streaming down her face. "Don't apologize, Gunner. We've had a good life together. Whatever happens, we face it together. I'm just worried about Mikhail."

In the dim light, they saw the glint of a weapon. Blondie's breath caught in her throat, and Gunner's grip tightened on the arms of the chair. They thought of their son and silently prayed that he would find peace and justice. Blondie closed her eyes, a final tear slipping down her cheek. Gunner took one last look at Blondie, the love of his life, the Russian soldier he had met after the crew of Hometown Gal parachuted to safety and smiled affectionately.

A loud sound echoed through the room. Blondie slumped. Another loud sound echoed through the room, and everything went dark.

CHAPTER 2

Just a week before the intruders tragically ended the lives of Blondie and Gunner, Gunner awoke in a daze, the sun's early morning rays peeking through the trees. He looked frazzled, perhaps still feeling the effects of his recurrent nightmares. Blondie lay by his side, sound asleep. Gunner stood quietly, dressed, and strolled slowly into the kitchen.

Like any other day, Gunner started to make breakfast while looking anxiously around the room. The fruity aroma of fresh brewing coffee permeated the room. He paused, if only for a moment, fixated on the calendar affixed to a peg board and the clock above the small desk behind him. He smiled and became lost in time. It was as if 2012 was 1945 again, and the Hometown Gal crew was preparing for their last mission. Memories flooded his mind—the sounds of engines roaring, the weight of his gear, the camaraderie, and fear. These memories soon vanished when he heard the sound of Blondie's soft footsteps approaching.

"Morning, beloved," she said, her voice gentle and warm. She touched his arm lightly, "Is everything alright?"

Gunner forced a smile. "Morning, honey. I'm just a bit lost in thought, I guess. Breakfast will be ready soon. Did you sleep well?"

Blondie gave him a knowing look but didn't press further. She knew better than to pry too deeply into the past, which he kept locked away.

"I slept soundly. Do you need any help?"

"No. Sit at the table, and I'll bring you a coffee. Once everything's ready, I'll roll the breakfast to the front porch so that we can take full advantage of the sunrise. It's beautiful this morning and warming up quickly, great for the grapes and the roses."

Blondie nodded affirmatively, sat down, and watched Gunner as he brought her coffee. The kitchen table, adorned with a bouquet of Blondie's award-winning red roses, seemed to soak up the love surrounding the couple.

Embracing Gunner's hands in hers, Blondie asked, "What does your week look like?"

"Pretty busy. I have a painting to finish, some work in the vineyard, and a trip to the gallery in Mendocino. I meet with Channing today and with Dutch at the end of the week. Are you excited about teaching quilt-making and rose cultivation classes at the Civic Center?"

"It is a busy one for us both. I'm excited to teach this week since both classes are full, although the thought of forty hours leaves little time for anything else. What's up with Channing and Dutch?"

"Channing asked me to meet him between Cloverdale and Mendocino to discuss his new novel and the dinner planned at his home during the Celebration. As for Dutch, I'll meet him at his gallery to discuss some paintings he's interested in."

The aroma that now filled the kitchen meant that breakfast was ready. Gunner carefully placed everything on the cart, including the pot of coffee, and with a smile, passed by Blondie, casually picking up her coffee cup and pointing her to the front porch.

Gunner gazed out the window, a warm smile spreading across his face as he took in the sight of the blooming rose garden. Turning to Blondie, he said, "Another splendid morning in the Valley. This scene always remains the same. I just get lost in love looking at your rose garden. It's even more beautiful this year, like you are, honey."

"Gunner, you always make me feel special, ever since my eyes met yours so many years ago. Who would have thought that a world war would unite us, and a cold war would never keep us apart?"

Blondie sat at the small table before the French doors to their bedroom. At the same time, Gunner arranged breakfast, poured Blondie and himself a glass of orange juice, topped off Blondie's coffee cup, and sat beside her.

"Let's eat before our breakfast gets cold and sit here enjoying the fragrance of the roses and the sight of those luscious grapes awakening to Mother Nature's call. Soon, we'll change our priorities to picking the vineyard clean and making our reserve pinot noir."

"Darling, do you think Mikhail will ever change? Will he settle down and start a family?"

"I hope so."

"I hope so, too. Mikhail's never been the same since he broke up with Ellie in high school. He was always looking for love but never truly finding it. I hate to think he'll remain an eligible bachelor all his life."

"Don't be too concerned. One day, he might find the love of his life like I did." With that, Gunner kissed Blondie, wrapped his arms around her, and whispered, "Love always finds a way."

CHAPTER 3

Gunner slowly went down the driveway in his SUV, the crunch of gravel beneath the tires echoing his uncertain thoughts. Soon, he found himself at the exit to Cloverdale off of U.S. Route 101. Lost in thought—or at least so it appeared—his keen eyes glinted with impending fear. Despite the many days he had spent in Cloverdale, he still admired the small town as he drove through it toward CA-128 West. The rolling hills and vineyards, historic buildings, and numerous art galleries painted a picturesque backdrop, even as unease settled in his mind.

He turned on the radio, seeking a distraction from his swirling thoughts. Just as he navigated the somewhat treacherous curves at the beginning of CA-128 West, one of his favorite 40's songs engulfed him in a way it never had before. The haunting melody and cryptic lyrics resonated deeply, stirring emotions he couldn't quite place. Somewhat confused, Gunner's hands tightened around the steering wheel. He appeared in a trance for a moment, the road ahead blurring into a mosaic of colors.

His calm demeanor was suddenly interrupted by the shrill ring of his phone. He shook his head to clear the fog as he answered.

"Good morning, Gunner. How close are you to our rendezvous point? I'm here waiting for you," Channing's clear and grounding voice said, interrupting Gunner's reverie and bringing him back to the present moment.

"Channing, you're a lifesaver. I almost drove off the road because I seemed to be hypnotized by my favorite song, and your call snapped me out of it," Gunner admitted, a hint of embarrassment in his tone.

"What, a song hypnotized you? You've got to be kidding!" Channing's laughter bubbled through the speaker, lightening Gunner's mood.

"I'm not. I should be at your location within 25 minutes," Gunner replied, glancing at the clock on the dashboard.

"I got us a small table outside, nearest to the chardonnay vineyard. The closest table to us will be about a hundred feet away. See you in 25."

"See you soon," Gunner said, ending the call. He turned off the radio, focusing entirely on the winding road ahead. The scenic route took him through Anderson Valley, where the late morning light filtered through the canopy of ancient redwoods, casting dappled shadows on the road. He took a deep breath, inhaling the earthy scent of the forest mingled with the subtle fragrance of blooming wildflowers.

Soon, he found himself at a small, picturesque vineyard in Anderson Valley. He parked, gathered up the picnic basket next to him, and walked down the path to Channing's table. The vineyard was serene, rows of neatly trellised vines stretching into the distance, heavy with clusters of ripening grapes.

"Hello, Gunner. I'm glad you made it in one piece. It's good to see that this beautiful vineyard doesn't hypnotize you," Channing greeted him with a smile, rising to give him a reassuring hug.

Gunner chuckled, "I think I'll be fine as long as there's no background music."

They settled at the table, a light breeze rustling the leaves of the nearby vines. Gunner opened the picnic basket, revealing an assortment of cheeses, fresh bread, and a bottle of Blondie's

Vineyard's finest Pinot.

"This looks amazing," Channing said, his eyes lighting up. "You always know how to make things special."

They clinked their glasses together, the crisp, purplish wine catching the sunlight. As they sipped, Gunner's expression grew serious.

"Channing, there's something we need to discuss," he began, his voice low and steady.

Channing's heart skipped a beat. The idyllic setting and the brief moment of peace seemed to fade as the weight of reality settled back in. He set down his glass and looked at Gunner, ready for whatever came next.

Gunner looked around as if someone was watching them. He peered back and forth and even stood up, scanning the surrounding vineyard. The rows of vines seemed to stretch endlessly, offering both a sense of isolation and exposure.

"What is it, Gunner?" Channing asked, concern evident in his voice.

Gunner sat back down, leaning closer. "I've been noticing things—people following me, strange calls. I believe someone is watching us."

Channing's eyes widened. "Are you sure? Here?"

"I don't know," Gunner admitted, glancing over his shoulder again. "But I can't shake the feeling. We need to be careful."

Channing nodded, his mind racing. "What do we do now?"

"We stay alert and stick to the plan," Gunner said, his voice firm. "But first, let's enjoy this meal. We'll talk about what's coming."

They resumed their lunch, the tension hanging in the air as palpable as the aroma of the vineyard around them. The picturesque setting now seemed to hold a sense of foreboding, a stark contrast to the peaceful moment they had shared just minutes before.

Gunner leaned back in his chair, looked at Channing, and said, "Before we discuss anything, let's top off lunch with a bottle of sweet wine and chocolates."

"That sounds great. I'll go to the tasting room while you sit back and relax." Channing calmly stated.

Channing got up, acknowledged Gunner's request, and strolled back to the small building, welcoming guests for wine tastings, food, and bottles to be purchased. Meanwhile, Gunner collected his thoughts and sketched the scene before him, taking out a small sketch book. Lost in his work, he captured the rolling vineyards and the gentle leaves swaying in the breeze. The act of drawing calmed him, grounding him in the present moment. Finally, he heard Channing's footsteps approaching the table, bringing him back to the reality of their situation.

"I'm back. How's the sketch going?" Channing asked, setting down the wine and chocolates.

"Such beauty in vineyards. I love to sketch in charcoal before I paint. This might be the last sketch that I do," Gunner replied, his voice tinged with melancholy.

"What? The last sketch? What do you mean?"

"We face a tenuous situation at best, and at worst, it's a death spiral, one that I don't want you to get caught up in," Gunner said, his eyes meeting Channing's with determination and fear.

Gunner's steel blue eyes focused on Channing's sad look as he secretively removed a small envelope from the basket at his side.

"What's this? Channing's mannerisms indicated that he didn't want to know.

"It's a gift. Open it up. You'll see."

Channing took a small knife and slowly opened the

envelope, revealing a letter. He started to read the letter out loud.

"Don't! Just read it to yourself, and you'll know what this meeting was about," Gunner interjected.

"Okay."

Channing slowly read the letter to himself while stealing glances at Gunner.

"Now I know why you said a death spiral. Is there no other way out?"

"No, not for me and not for Blondie. The end has to be faced to ensure a new beginning. Your challenge will be to ensure that the new beginning matures into the right ending. I have full confidence in you."

Channing nodded, his head slumped, and his eyes again met Gunner's.

"Thank you for the vote of confidence. I'll make sure Mickey gets what he's supposed to at the right time. Are you certain the plan will play out in the way you think it will?"

Slowly turning away from Channing, Gunner smiled as he watched the afternoon's golden rays bring the vineyards around him to life. He then looked back at Channing, who immediately grabbed a small metal box on the table, lit the letter with his lighter, and deposited it into the box.

"Yes," Gunner said. With that, Channing and Gunner embraced, a silent understanding passing between them. They cleaned up the table and returned to their vehicles. Gunner drove back to Healdsburg, and Channing made his way toward Mendocino.

CHAPTER 4

Gunner felt the world's weight on his shoulders as he drove back to Healdsburg, his thoughts dwelling more on the past than the short future he anticipated. Memories flooded his mind, each a vivid reminder of the choices that had led him and Blondie to this point from 1945. The hope and ambition that filled their hearts, the blossoming love, the friendships forged in the skies over Europe and then lost on American soil, and the moments of triumph now felt distant and hollow.

The road ahead blurred as he navigated the all-too-familiar route. The sun began its descent from its apex, casting different shadows across the vineyards. The beauty of the landscape, with its rolling hills and lush vineyards, once a source of inspiration, now felt like a poignant reminder of everything that was slipping away. The golden light filtering through the trees played tricks on his eyes, merging past and present into a confusing tapestry of regret, resolve, joy, and pain.

Every mile that brought him closer to Healdsburg also brought him nearer to the end of his and Blondie's lives. The echoes of past conversations, laughter, and unfulfilled promises haunted him, each a ghostly whisper in the car's silence. He thought about Blondie, their shared life, and the love that had sustained them through everything. He thought about Michael and his future, one he knew would be fraught with danger but, if met correctly, would mature him beyond his years.

The responsibility now borne by Gunner weighed heavily

on him, pressing down with a tightening force. He took a deep breath, then another, trying to shake off the melancholy that clung to him like a wet t-shirt as he approached Healdsburg. Once a beacon of familiarity, the town now felt like a stranger. Just like that fateful March day in 1945, there was another mission to complete, one that required unwavering focus and determination.

As he neared home, Gunner stopped at the Palm Tree Inn to see Lance and Judy, the owners of the bed and breakfast and two lifelong friends. In less than two weeks, they would entertain the relatives of the crew of Hometown Gal during the anniversary celebration of Russian settlers first landing in Northern California two hundred years ago, advertised as the 200th Anniversary Celebration. Gunner parked his car in the lot next to the Inn and started walking to the path that led to its front steps. Before he reached the water tower at the start of the path, Lance burst out the door and greeted him with a hearty wave.

"Hello, Gunner! I didn't expect to see you today. Aren't you and Blondie spending the weekend with us while you work on your house? What gives? You look like you've got the world's weight on your shoulders."

Gunner managed a smile. "I just thought I'd stop by to say hello and get a taste of that fine Zinfandel you bottled last year. Blondie's teaching this week at the community college, and I just had lunch with Channing."

Lance's eyes twinkled. "Well, in that case, make your way to my cellar. I'll open a bottle, pour three glasses, and find Judy. We can sit on the porch and take in the view."

The two men, one in his early 80s and the other in his early 70s, walked slowly to the cellar. Moments later, they emerged, somewhat gracefully making their way up the stairs to the front porch, where Lance called out for Judy.

"I hear you, Lance," Judy's cheerful voice from inside said.

"I'll be out there in a couple of minutes. Do you guys want anything to munch on while you drink?"

Lance glanced at Gunner with a grin. "How about some of those famous cheese straws of yours?"

Judy laughed. "Coming right up! You boys settle in and enjoy the view."

As the men sat down, Lance poured the wine, the deep red liquid catching the late afternoon light. Gunner took a deep breath, savoring the familiar, comforting aroma of the vineyard.

"This wine is what I needed," Gunner said, lifting his glass. "Here's to good friends and good wine."

"Cheers to that!" Lance replied, clinking his glass with Gunner's just as Judy appeared with a plate of cheese straws. Her smile was as warm as the sun that covered the vineyard.

"Here you go, boys. Fresh from the oven," Judy said, setting the plate down.

"So, Gunner, tell us more about this lunch with Channing. It must have been important to bring you out here looking so serious." Lance asked with a not-so-serious expression.

Gunner took a sip of the Zinfandel, letting the rich flavors roll over his tongue before speaking. "It was important. We discussed the plans for the Celebration, and I had to finalize a few details with him. A lot is riding on this event, and I want everything perfect for the families coming in."

Judy nodded, understanding the weight of the occasion. "It's a big responsibility, but if anyone can handle it, it's you. You've always had a knack for bringing people together."

Lance leaned back in his chair, a nostalgic look in his eyes. "Remember the first time we all met? It was at that little airfield outside of town. Who would've thought we'd still be here, all these years later, sharing wine and getting ready for what should be a fantastic Celebration?"

Gunner chuckled. "Seems like a lifetime ago. But here we are, and I wouldn't have it any other way."

They sat in pleasant silence, enjoying the wine and the view. The vineyard stretched out before them, a patchwork of green and gold under the late afternoon sun. Birds chirped softly in the distance, and the gentle rustle of leaves in the breeze added a soothing backdrop to their thoughts. As the afternoon wore on, the conversation turned to lighter topics—old stories, shared jokes, and plans for the upcoming Celebration. The laughter and camaraderie warmed Gunner's heart, easing his burden, if only for a little while, and reminding him of the unwavering support he had from his friends.

Finally, as the sun continued its journey to the west and shadows started to appear in the flower garden along the path, Gunner stood up, stretching his legs. "I should get going. Thank you both for the wine and the company."

Lance and Judy stood as well, hugging Gunner tightly. "Take care, Gunner," Judy said softly. "And remember, we're always here if you need anything."

"Thanks, Judy. I know," Gunner replied, a hint of a smile touching his lips. "See you both soon."

As he drove away from the Palm Tree Inn, the weight on his shoulders felt just a little bit lighter, bolstered by the love and support of his friends. The road ahead was still uncertain, but with friends like Lance and Judy by his side, he knew he could face whatever came his way. The trip from the Inn to the Gabbro's home lasted less than 10 minutes. With Blondie expected to be home within an hour, Gunner had just enough time to cook dinner in the oven and wait for her on the porch facing the road. Around 5:00 pm, he spotted Blondie's minivan moving slowly up the gravel road to her appointed parking space in front of the workshop. He walked out to greet her with a hug and kiss.

"Hi, sweetheart! How were the classes today?"

"Exhausting, but wonderful. A great group of students paid close attention to everything I lectured about, and many asked excellent questions. I look forward to the rest of the week. How was your day? How did lunch go with Channing?"

"A perfect day for me. Channing stepped up and found an excellent spot for lunch, and on the way back, I stopped over at the Inn for a drink and cheese straws with Lance and Judy."

"I'm surprised you stopped to see them, given that we'll be there this weekend. Did you call the contractor to see if they're coming on Friday?"

"I did. Yes, Placer Contractors are starting Friday late afternoon and finishing up mid-day Sunday."

"Perfect. What did Lance, Judy, and you talk about?"

"Nothing too important. They asked me about my meeting with Channing, and then we just reminisced about when we first met. You look tired. Let me take your briefcase. Go in, freshen up, and relax on the back porch. Dinner should be ready in about 30 minutes."

"Sounds great."

Gunner took her briefcase in one hand and held her other hand as they walked up the front porch and through the front door. A single tear flowed down from his right eye, unnoticed by Blondie, as she headed inside.

CHAPTER 5

As the evening unfolded with a 2009 Reserve Pinot from Blondie's Vineyard complementing their dinner, a sudden change in Blondie's demeanor cast a shadow over the peaceful scene. Her once cheerful eyes darkened, and her smile gave way to a troubled expression, sparking concern in Gunner.

"Blondie, is everything alright?" Gunner asked, setting his glass down and leaning forward.

Blondie sighed, her fingers tracing the rim of her wine glass. "I've been thinking a lot about the future, about everything we've been through and what's coming next," she said, her voice laced with an uncharacteristic doom mentality. The uncertainty of what lies ahead was weighing heavily on her mind.

Gunner reached across the table, taking her hand in his. "Talk to me. What's on your mind?"

Blondie took a deep breath, her eyes meeting Gunner's. "I've been feeling this growing sense of dread. I can't shake the feeling that something bad is going to happen. It's like a storm cloud hovering over us, getting darker and closer. I can't explain why I feel this way."

Gunner squeezed her hand gently. "I understand. We've been through a lot, and it's natural to worry. But whatever happens, we'll face it together."

Blondie nodded, but the worry in her eyes remained. "I know, but it's not just about us. It's about Mikhail and everything we've built. I want to protect it all, but things are slipping out of our control."

Gunner stood up, walking around the table to pull her into a comforting embrace. "How so? Nothing is out of control; if it ever was, we'd find a way to regain control. We always do; if we need help, many folks will help us. We're not alone."

Blondie rested her head on his shoulder, drawing strength from his presence. "Thank you, Gunner. I just needed to hear that."

They stood there momentarily, holding onto each other, their hearts pounding in sync with the growing uncertainty they now both felt. The fading glow of the sun and the lingering aroma of lamb and wine contrasted sharply with their shared anxiety.

"Let's take it one step at a time. We've got a big celebration coming up, and we must focus on making it a success. After that, we'll deal with whatever comes our way." Gunner's voice was filled with determination, a testament to their resilience in the face of uncertainty.

Blondie managed a small smile. "You're right. One step at a time."

They cleared the back porch table together, slow and deliberate, as if savoring the mundane task, and walked into the kitchen. Each dish they washed and dried felt like a small victory against the encroaching darkness.

The conversation became lighter as they settled into the living room with another glass of wine. They reminisced about their favorite moments from the past and shared dreams for the future, even as a silent understanding lingered between them. The night wore on, and despite the earlier tension, they found comfort in each other's presence, ready to face whatever challenges lay ahead.

Morning came quickly, and after a long night of

conversation, the challenge they faced kept buzzing until they both awoke. After a quick breakfast, Gunner drove Blondie to the start of her first class.

"Thanks, darling. Pick me up at 5:00 pm. We could then go to dinner at Phillipi's. I'll call Antonio on my first break and get a reservation for our favorite outdoor table. Does that sound good?

"Sure does. See you at 5:00 pm sharp."

As Blondie hurriedly rushed into the building, Gunner answered a call from Alexander Federov.

"Good morning, Vincent."

"Good morning, Alexander. What can I do for you?"

"Please meet me at the location I will text you as soon as you can. It's urgent. Thank you."

Before Gunner could respond, Alexander abruptly ended the call. Perplexed and uneasy, Gunner stared at his phone, awaiting Alexander's text.

Five tense minutes later, his phone buzzed. The message appeared on the screen:

"Meet me at the table where you and Channing had lunch yesterday afternoon. I'll explain everything when you get there. Hurry, please!"

Gunner's heart pounded as he processed the message. Without wasting a moment, he sped off, the urgency gnawing at him like a persistent ache. The drive to the Anderson Valley vineyard stretched interminably, every second feeling like an eternity. The blur of passing scenery barely registered as his mind swirled with troubling possibilities, each more concerning than the last. Could Alexander be in danger? Had something gone terribly wrong since his lunch with Channing?

As he approached the familiar table, he scanned the area, noting the absence of anyone around except Alexander, who sported a grave expression, his eyes darting around as if being watched. Gunner slowed his gait and stopped momentarily, anticipating danger lurking in the vineyard.

"Alexander," Gunner greeted, sliding into the seat opposite him.

"Vincent, thank you for coming so quickly," Alexander replied, his voice low and urgent. "We don't have much time. There's been a development—something we didn't foresee."

Gunner leaned in, his pulse quickening. "What's happened?"

Alexander handed him a folder, his hands trembling slightly. "Read this. It's all in there. We have a narrow window in which to act, and every second counts."

Gunner opened the folder, quickly scanning the documents. The gravity of the situation became apparent, and his eyes widened. "This changes everything," he muttered, looking up at Alexander.

"Yes, it does," Alexander confirmed, his gaze even more intense. "We need to move fast and be precise. If we don't, the consequences will be catastrophic."

Gunner nodded, his mind already shifting into action mode. "What's the plan?"

Alexander leaned forward, outlining the strategy in hushed tones. Gunner listened intently, his earlier perplexity giving way to determination. The puzzle pieces were falling into place, and the path ahead, though dangerous, was becoming apparent. As they finalized their plans, the gravity of their mission settled between them, unspoken but understood. They were racing against time, and failure was not an option.

Gunner stood up, clasping Alexander's shoulder. "We'll make it through this. We have to."

Alexander nodded, a flicker of hope in his eyes. "Stay sharp, Vincent. We're counting on you."

With that, Gunner burned the folder's contents just as Channing had done the day before, ensuring no evidence remained. He then turned and walked away, the weight of urgency pressing heavily on him. The game was approaching its end faster than he thought, and he knew he had to quickly finish the document that would soon be in Channing's hands.

Wasting no time, Gunner raced home, continually checking his rearview mirror for any signs of a tail. Upon arriving, he immediately entered his workshop, locking the door behind him. His heart pounded as he moved quickly to the back of the workshop. He removed some books from the shelf, slid open a small door, and took out a device resembling a cell phone with dials. With a quick, practiced motion, he turned the dials and glanced at the now functioning screen, confirming that no one had entered the workshop or their home.

Gunner let out a small breath of relief before opening the door to the wine cellar. He walked in, turned on the lights, and closed the door behind him. The cool, musty air of the cellar enveloped him as he used his device to set an alarm and open another door at the back of the cellar. It creaked open, revealing a secret room known only to Gunner. The familiar scent of aged wood and faint traces of wine filled the air, grounding him momentarily in the midst of the tension.

Gunner calmly sat down at a large desk covered with family photos, each one a reminder of the love and life he cherished. His fingers brushed over the frames, pausing on two significant photos from his days in the Army Air Forces. The first photo showed the nine crew members of Hometown Gal who survived their last mission, along with the five Russian soldiers who had guarded them. Two of those soldiers were women, one being his true love, Blondie. He smiled softly at the memory, her determined eyes and the fierce strength she carried.

The second photo, taken at the Amendola Airfield in Foggia, Italy, captured the entire crew standing in front of the left side of Hometown Gal, accompanied by Colonel Harrington and his second in command, Major Hastings. The pride in their faces was evident, a testament to their courage and camaraderie. Gunner could almost hear the hum of the engines and the distant echo of their laughter, a stark contrast to the silence of the room he now occupied.

He took a deep breath, the scent of aged wood mingling with the faint aroma of paper and ink, grounding him. These photos weren't just memories; they were a testament to the life he had lived and the people he had loved and lost. He closed his eyes letting the images of those days wash over him. After another deep breath, he opened his eyes, feeling a sense of calm determination. He picked up his pen and began to write, capturing the essence of a time long past.

With each stroke of his pen, the memories flowed more freely. His hand moved steadily across the paper, each word a bridge to the past. He could almost hear the roar of engines and smell the interior of his B-17 bomber. The thrill of daytime bombing missions, the bond with his crew, and the haunting silence after each mission came rushing back. The page began to fill with the essence of those turbulent yet defining days.

CHAPTER 6

I remember it all too vividly. War broke out throughout Europe, and every day, we heard news stories on the radio and read about the war in newspapers. The world was on edge, and young men, including myself, felt an overwhelming urge to enlist.

I dreamed of being a flyboy, piloting fighters or bombers. The allure of the skies, the thought of soaring above the chaos, and the hope of making a difference drove me. I envisioned myself in the cockpit, the roar of the engines in my ears, and the thrill of missions that would tip the scales in our favor. The camaraderie among the airmen, the honor of serving my country, and the chance to be part of something greater than myself were powerful motivators.

The other day, I broached the subject with my soon-to-be fiancée, Marya Skowski, the most beautiful girl in Hamtramck. Her eyes widened with concern as I spoke of my desire to enlist. "Vincent," she said, her voice trembling slightly, "the thought of you flying into danger terrifies me, but I understand why you feel you must go."

Marya was a pillar of strength and understanding; her support meant the world to me. We spent that evening walking through the streets of Hamtramck, the vibrant Polish community bustling around us. Still, all I could think about was the uncertainty of the future. As the night ended, under the soft glow of streetlights, I got on my knees, pulled out the engagement ring I had bought the week before, and sheepishly asked, "Marya, would you marry me?"

"Yes, on one condition," she replied, her eyes shining with determination.

"What condition?" I asked, my heart pounding.

"That you promise me you'll make it back."

I promised her I would return, that our dreams of a life together would not be forgotten. Then she said something that made me pause.

"When you return, we'll get married and start raising a family."

"What do you mean? I thought we'd get married right away."

Marya smiled softly, a hint of sadness in her eyes. "Vincent, I want our joy-filled wedding day not to be overshadowed by the war. I want you to come back to me, safe and whole, so we can truly begin our life together without the fear of separation hanging over us."

Her words struck a chord deep within me. I realized she was right; our wedding should be a celebration of our love, not rushed or marred by the looming shadow of war. I nodded, understanding her perspective. "I promise, Marya. I'll return to you, and we'll have the best wedding and the life we've always dreamed of."

With that promise, we sealed our commitment to each other. As I held Marya close, I felt a renewed sense of purpose. I knew that I had a reason to fight and survive no matter the challenges. Marya's love and our future became my guiding light in the darkest times.

The following day, I broke the news about proposing to Marya and my desire to enlist. My family gathered around the breakfast table, their expressions shifting from curiosity to shock as I spoke. My mother's eyes filled with tears, her hands trembling as she clutched her apron. "Wincenty, are you sure about this?" she asked, her voice a mixture of fear and pride.

"Yes, Mom," I replied, sounding more confident than I felt. "I need to do this. It's something I must do for myself, Marya, and our country."

My stoic father, who had seen his share of hardships, nodded. "We're proud of you, son. Just make sure you come back to us in one piece."

My sisters, younger and more prone to expressing their emotions, clung to me, their tears soaking into my shirt. "Don't go, Vinny," they pleaded, their voices small and fearful. "We don't want to lose you."

I hugged them tightly, trying to reassure them with promises I hoped I could keep. "I'll be back," I said firmly. "I promise."

After breakfast, Mom cornered me outside. She knew that I didn't tell everyone the whole story.

"What's on your mind, Wincenty?"

I hated it when she called Wincenty. I wanted everyone to call me Vince after Vincent "Vince" DiMaggio since he, like me, played center field—only he played in the big leagues. But I couldn't bring myself to correct her. She was my mother, after all.

"Mom, it's just… I need to do something meaningful. Sitting here while the world is at war feels wrong. And I want to make Marya proud."

"I know, but something else is bothering you."

"Mom, I'd like to get married immediately, but Marya wants to wait until I return."

Mom looked at me with understanding eyes, her expression softening. "She wants to make sure you come back safe. She wants your wedding day to be a joyful celebration, not overshadowed by worry."

"I get that," I said, frustration edging my voice. "But it's hard. I want to know Marya's mine, and I'm hers before I go."

She placed a gentle hand on my shoulder. "Wincenty, love isn't just about a ceremony. It's about the promises you make and keep, whether you're here or across the world. Marya's love for you won't change whether you're married now or later. Focus on coming back to her. That's what matters most."

I nodded, feeling a bit more at ease. "Thanks, Mom. I'll do everything I can to come back and make her proud."

CHAPTER 7

The day I enlisted was bittersweet. The pride of serving my country was now tempered by my sadness about leaving Marya and the life we had begun to build. As I stood in line with other young men, I couldn't help but notice the mix of emotions on their faces—determination, fear, and hope. We were all bound by a common purpose, yet we each carried personal stories and loved ones we were leaving behind.

The recruiting station was a small, bustling office on Main Street, sandwiched between a diner and a hardware store. Vibrant posters proclaiming, "Victory Begins in the Air", "The Sky's the Limit!", and "Fly with the Army Air Forces" plastered the walls. A large American flag hung prominently behind the main desk, and the air was thick with the scent of fresh coffee and the murmur of conversation.

A tall, stern-looking sergeant named Miller staffed the desk. He was a veteran of the First World War, with a chest full of medals and a demeanor that commanded respect. Young men, clutching their paperwork and hoping to be selected for the prestigious Army Air Forces, lined up in anticipation and anxiety. When it was my turn, I stepped forward with nervous excitement. Sergeant Miller looked up, his focused eyes scanning me from head to toe.

"Name?" the sergeant barked.

"Wincenty Gabrowski, sir. But everyone calls me Vince," I replied, trying to sound confident.

Sergeant Miller nodded and began filling out a form. "What makes you think you've got what it takes to be part of the Army Air Forces, Wincenty?"

I straightened up. "I've always dreamed of flying, sir. I want to serve my country from the skies."

The sergeant studied me briefly before handing me a stack of papers. "Fill these out, and then we'll get you through the initial assessments."

The initial assessments were rigorous. Along with other hopefuls, I underwent a battery of tests. These included physical exams, where doctors checked our vision, hearing, and overall physical fitness. We also took written exams to assess our intellectual capabilities and underwent psychological evaluations to determine our mental resilience.

I passed the physical exams with flying colors. Thanks to my part-time job working in the lumber yard and my love of sports, I was in good shape. The written exams were challenging, especially the Aviation Cadet Qualifying Exam, which assessed my intellectual and cognitive abilities through mathematics, mechanical comprehension, and spatial awareness tests. The psychological evaluation was the most daunting, with questions designed to test my decision-making skills, emotional stability, and stress tolerance. I found out later that these tests weeded out those who couldn't handle the pressures of being a pilot.

After the assessments, there was a period of waiting. They told us to return home and await our orders. Days felt like weeks as I went about my daily life, working and spending time with Marya while dreaming of the day I would take to the skies. Finally, on April 14th, the letter arrived. I tore it open with trembling hands. The Army Air Forces accepted me and listed my reporting date for basic training at Maxwell Field in Alabama as May 1st. Pride, anticipation, and sadness filled my heart as I faced the separation from Marya.

The night before I left for training, Marya and I decided to spend the entire evening together, cherishing every moment. We met at our favorite spot, a small park in the heart of the city. The trees' delicate blossom petals drifted down like snowflakes.

"Marya, look at these blossoms," I said, taking her hand. "They're beautiful, just like you."

Marya's eyes looked sorrowful, but she still smiled. "Vincent, I'm going to miss you so much. Every time I see these blossoms, I'll think of you."

We walked through the park in silence for a while, our hands tightly clasped. The familiar surroundings felt different as if the weight of what would come had changed the air around us. As the sun set, casting an amber glow over the city, we found a bench and sat down.

"Vincent," Marya began, her voice trembling slightly, "I've been thinking about the future a lot. I'm so proud of you for following your dreams, but I'm scared too. What if something happens to you?"

I took her hands in mine and looked deeply into her eyes. "Marya, I promise you, I'll do everything I can to return home to you. We'll get through this, and when I return, we'll have the wedding we've always dreamed of."

A tear rolled down her cheek, and I gently wiped it away. "You're the love of my life, Marya. Nothing will ever change that."

She leaned her head on my shoulder, and we sat there for a long time, watching the stars grow brighter as the night progressed. The city lights twinkled around us, creating a beautiful contrast with the darkening sky.

"Do you remember the first time we met?" Marya asked softly.

I smiled, vividly recalling that day. "Of course I do. You were standing in line at the bakery, and I accidentally bumped into you. You dropped your bread, and I felt so bad that I bought you a new loaf."

She laughed, and the sound was like music to my ears. "And then you asked if you could walk me home, and we talked the whole way. I knew right then that you were special."

We talked for hours, reminiscing about all the moments we had shared—the laughter, the tears, the dreams we had for our future. As the night grew colder, I wrapped my arm around her, trying to hold on to the warmth of our love.

"Promise me again that you'll come back," she whispered, barely audible.

"I promise," I said, embracing her tightly. "We'll get through this, and when I come back, we'll never be apart again."

We stood in front of her house, the porch light casting a soft glow around us. I could see the pain in her eyes and the unwavering love and faith she had in me. I kissed her gently, trying to pour all my love and reassurance into that one moment.

"Marya, I love you more than anything in this world. Keep this with you," I said, handing her a small locket. "It has a picture of us inside. Whenever you miss me, hold it and know that I'm thinking of you."

She opened the locket and smiled through her tears. "I love you too, Vincent. Be safe and come back to me. I also have something for you."

With that, she gave me two framed pictures of her, and with one last kiss, I turned and walked away, my heart heavy with the knowledge of our impending separation. But I knew our love would carry us through, no matter how far apart we were.

The following day was even more challenging. My family gathered in the living room, the air thick with unspoken words and raw emotions. My mother, always the strong one, was the first to speak.

"Wincenty, take care of yourself," she said, her voice wavering. "I'll be praying for you every day."

I hugged her tightly, feeling her tears on my shoulder. "I will, Mom. I promise."

My father, usually a man of few words, pulled me into a bear hug. "Make us proud, son. And come back home."

"I will, Dad."

My sisters clung to me, their faces wet with tears. "Don't go, Vinny," they sobbed. "We don't want to lose you."

I knelt to their level, trying to keep my voice steady. "I'll be back before you know it. Just take care of each other while I'm gone."

As I stepped out the door, my father called me back, his voice unusually soft. "Vincent, can I talk to you for a minute?"

I nodded and followed him to the kitchen, where he closed the door behind us. He took a deep breath, his eyes avoiding mine.

"Vincent, there's something you need to know," he began, his voice heavy with emotion. "Your mother... she's been diagnosed with stomach cancer."

The words hit me like a punch to the gut. "What? When did this happen?" I asked, my voice trembling.

"A few weeks ago," he said, his eyes finally meeting mine. "I didn't want to burden you with it before you left, but you deserve to know. The doctors are doing what they can, but it's serious."

I felt a wave of guilt and fear wash over me. "Why didn't you tell me sooner?"

"We didn't want to distract you from your dreams," he said, placing a hand on my shoulder. "Your mother insisted on it. She wants you to follow your path, no matter what."

I swallowed hard, trying to process the news. "I... I don't know what to say."

"Just promise me you'll stay strong and focused," my father said, his voice breaking slightly. "Your mother needs to know that you're out there doing what you love. It gives her strength."

I nodded, tears stinging my eyes. "I promise, Dad. I'll make you both proud."

We hugged tightly, and then I returned to the living room. My mother looked at me with a sad but proud smile.

As I walked down the steps, the weight of their love and concern pressed down on me. I turned back one last time, taking in their faces, and then I headed towards my future, determined to honor their hopes and dreams.

CHAPTER 8

The bus ride to Maxwell Field felt like the beginning of a grand adventure. As we rumbled through the countryside, the excitement and nervous energy among the recruits were noticeable. I sat next to Anthony "Tony" Kowalski, from Chicago. Tony was a wiry guy with a quick smile and a knack for cracking jokes, which made the long trip more bearable. The rhythmic hum of the bus engine, the sight of the passing fields, and the fresh, earthy smell of the countryside all added to the anticipation of what was to come.

"Vincent, have you ever seen a place like Maxwell Field?" Tony asked, leaning back in his seat.

"I've heard stories," I replied, looking out the window as the landscape blurred. "But I guess we're about to find out firsthand. Also, call me Vince."

"I hear it's like nothing we've ever seen. My uncle told me they've got planes lined up for miles and the best instructors in the country. We're going to be part of something big, Vince."

"Yeah," I said, feeling excited and nervous. It's hard to believe we're actually doing this."

Tony nudged me with his elbow. "Believe it, buddy. We're going to be pilots. Can you imagine? Flying high above the clouds, looking down on the world. It's going to be incredible!"

I nodded, trying to match his enthusiasm. "Yeah, incredible."

As the bus rolled on, Tony's chatter filled the air. He talked about his family back in Chicago, his dreams of flying, and the adventures he hoped to have. His optimism was infectious, and I got caught up in the excitement despite my nerves.

"Do you think we'll all make it?" he asked suddenly, his tone more serious.

I shrugged. "I don't know. Folks say it's tough, but we've made it this far, right?"

"We've got this, Vince. No matter what, we're in it together," Tony declared, his eyes filled with determination. His words echoed our unbreakable bond, instilling a sense of unity and strength in the face of the challenges ahead.

As we neared Maxwell Field, the sight that greeted us was nothing short of awe-inspiring. The airfield sprawled out before us, a vast expanse of runways, hangars, and barracks. The American flag, proudly waving over the main entrance, symbolized the pride and duty that awaited us, leaving us in awe of the journey we were about to embark on.

Maxwell Field buzzed with activity. Planes roared overhead, practicing takeoffs and landings, while ground crews moved with precision, tending to the aircraft. Recruits marched in neat rows, their cadence echoing through the crisp morning air. The sun glinted off the wings of the parked planes, casting sharp shadows on the tarmac. I felt a surge of excitement and pride, knowing that soon, I would be part of this vibrant, purposeful world.

We stepped off the bus, the hot Alabama sun beating down on us. Sergeant Sanders was there to greet us, his stern expression a reminder of the discipline and rigor that awaited.

"Welcome to Maxwell Field, gentlemen," he barked. "From this moment on, you are cadets in the Army Air Forces. You will eat, sleep, and breathe training. Is that understood?"

"Yes, sir!" we replied in unison, our voices strong and determined.

As we hustled to our barracks, Tony nudged me. "Can you believe it, Vince? We're here. We're going to be flyboys."

"Yeah, it's hard to believe," I said, seeing the planes and the bustling airfield. "But we've got a lot of work ahead of us."

The barracks were simple but functional, with rows of neatly made bunks and lockers. The smell of fresh linen and the sound of distant engines created a surreal atmosphere. Tony and I claimed adjacent bunks, quickly stowing our gear.

"So, are you ready for this?" Tony asked, flopping onto his bed.

"As ready as I'll ever be," I replied, feeling excitement and apprehension.

After a hearty meal in the mess hall that evening, we had a few moments of free time. Tony and I wandered over to the airfield, watching the planes as the sun set in a blaze of orange and pink.

"Ever wonder what it'll be like up there?" Tony asked.

"Every day," I said. "I can't wait to feel the controls in my hands, to see the world from above."

"We're gonna be the best damn pilots this field has ever seen, Vincent."

I laughed. "Damn right, we are."

As darkness fell, the airfield lights flickered on, casting a glow over the planes and runways. Field crickets filled the air, mingling with the distant hum of engines. It was a moment of peace before the storm of training that awaited us.

Back in the barracks, as I lay in my bunk, I thought about Marya, my family, and my promise to them. Soft snores filled the room, a comforting reminder that I wasn't alone on this journey.

"Goodnight, Tony," I whispered, feeling a sense of camaraderie and determination.

"Goodnight, Vince," he murmured back, half-asleep. "Tomorrow, we start making history."

With that thought, I closed my eyes, ready to embrace the challenges and adventures ahead at Maxwell Field.

CHAPTER 9

Basic training at Maxwell Field would be an intense, transformative experience. Every waking moment, the instructors thrust us into a world of discipline, physical exertion, and relentless instruction. Every day was a test of our limits, both physically and mentally.

The morning after we arrived, reveille sounded at 0500 hours, a blaring bugle call that shattered the pre-dawn silence. Tony groaned from the bunk beside mine as we stumbled out of bed and hurried to get dressed.

"Rise and shine, gentlemen!" Sergeant Sander's voice boomed through the barracks. "You've got five minutes to be outside in formation!"

We scrambled to get dressed, the rush of adrenaline waking us up faster than any cup of coffee could. Outside, the air was warm and humid, and the first light of dawn was beginning to peek over the horizon. We lined up in neat rows, standing at attention as Sergeant Sanders inspected us.

"Today, we're going to see what you cadets are made of," he announced, his eyes glinting with a mix of challenge and encouragement. "First up, a five-mile run. I want to see every one of you push yourselves to the limit. Let's move out!"

The run was grueling. The Alabama heat and humidity quickly became oppressive as the sun rose higher. Still, we pushed through, motivated by the desire to prove ourselves. Tony and I ran side by side, encouraging each other to keep going.

"Come on, Vince, just a little farther," Tony panted, sweat streaming down his face.

"We've got this," I replied, gritting my teeth against the fatigue. "No way we're falling behind."

After the run, we moved on to physical training exercises: push-ups, sit-ups, and obstacle courses—each drill designed to build strength and endurance. The training grounds were a hive of activity, with recruits pushing themselves and each other to the brink.

"Gabrowski, you call that a push-up?" Sergeant Sanders barked as he passed by. "Get your back straight and give me ten more!"

"Yes, sir!" I responded, adjusting my form and pushing through the additional reps.

Drenched in sweat and muscles aching, we headed to the mess hall for breakfast before the next training phase. The mess hall was filled with the clatter of trays and the hum of conversation as we wolfed down our food, knowing we'd need every bit of energy for the day ahead.

After breakfast, it was time for classroom instruction. We filed into a large lecture hall, taking our seats as the instructor began a lesson on aviation theory. Charts and diagrams lined the walls, and a model plane hung from the ceiling.

"Today, we're going to cover the basics of aerodynamics," the instructor began. "Understanding how your aircraft flies is just as important as knowing how to fly it. Pay attention! This knowledge could save your life."

The lessons were intense and detailed. We learned about lift, thrust, drag, and the various control surfaces of an aircraft. Despite the fatigue from the morning's physical training, we were all keenly focused, knowing that mastering this information was crucial.

During a break, Tony turned to me, puzzled. "You get all this. It's like a foreign language to me."

"It's a lot to take in," I admitted, "but we'll get there. We have to keep studying."

Flight training occurred in the afternoons. We marched to the airfield, where rows of training planes awaited. The sight of aircraft gleaming in the sunlight filled us with a renewed sense of purpose.

"Alright, cadets," Sergeant Sanders called out. "Today, you're going to start with taxiing and basic maneuvers. Listen to your instructors and follow their commands precisely. Safety is paramount."

My heart pounded as I climbed into the cockpit for the first time. The controls felt foreign under my hands, but the thrill of being in the pilot's seat was indescribable. The instructor behind me guided me through the pre-flight checks and basic procedures.

"Alright, Vince, ease the throttle forward," the instructor said. "Feel the plane respond. That's it, nice and smooth."

Taxiing down the runway, I felt a rush of adrenaline. Every movement of the controls translated into a response from the aircraft, and I realized just how much there was to learn.

The days merged into a rhythm of rigorous training and intense study. Each night, we collapsed into our bunks, exhausted but determined. The camaraderie among the recruits grew stronger daily as we shared our struggles and triumphs.

One evening, Tony spoke up as we sat around in the barracks after a particularly grueling day. "You know, this is the hardest thing I've ever done. But I wouldn't trade it for anything."

"Me neither," I agreed, feeling a deep camaraderie. "We're in this together. We're gonna make it through."

Sergeant Sanders' voice echoed in my mind as I drifted to

sleep, his words a constant reminder of our mission. "You're here to become the best. To protect and defend. Never forget that."

CHAPTER 10

The days wore on until the day of reckoning appeared — the day that we would hear the results of our latest evaluations and find out if we were going to be pilots. Once again, the familiar bugle call tore through the pre-dawn stillness. As I rolled out of my bunk and quickly dressed, I couldn't shake the gnawing feeling of anxiety that had settled in my gut over the past few days.

Tony grinned at me from the next bunk. "Hey Vince, today's the day. I can feel it. We're gonna make it!"

I forced a smile. "Yeah, Tony. We've got this."

The morning began as usual with a grueling five-mile run and physical training exercises under Sergeant Sanders's watchful eye. I pushed myself harder than ever, trying to focus on each step and each breath rather than the looming results. As usual, the run ended with the cadets drenched in sweat and panting in the Alabama heat. After breakfast, the cadets assembled in the main hall to hear the evaluation results announced. The atmosphere was thick with anticipation and nerves. My hands felt clammy, and I wiped them on my trousers, trying to calm the storm inside me.

Our flight instructor, Lieutenant Parker, stood at the front of the hall with a stack of papers. He carried a serious expression, and the room fell silent as he began calling out names.

"Anthony Kowalski," Parker called. Tony's name was one of the first. He stepped forward, confidently nodding to receive his evaluation results. Parker gave him a firm handshake and a rare smile. "Congratulations, Kowalski. You've made it to the next phase."

Tony returned to his seat, beaming. I clapped him on the back, trying to hide my nervousness. "I knew you'd make it," I said.

As the list continued, my heart pounded louder. I watched as other cadets received their results, some faces lighting up with joy, others tightening with disappointment. Finally, Parker called "Vincent Gabrowski."

I stood up, my legs feeling like lead, and walked to the front of the hall. Parker handed me my evaluation results, his face betraying nothing.

"See me after the meeting, Gabrowski," Parker said quietly.

Despite the sinking feeling in my heart, I straightened my shoulders. I knew what that meant, but I was determined not to let it break me.

After the meeting, I met with Lieutenant Parker in a small office. The atmosphere was tense; I felt the walls closing in around me. Every second stretched into an eternity as I waited for Parker to speak. The office was sparsely decorated, with a large wooden desk dominating the center. The desk was meticulously organized, with neat stacks of papers, a brass desk lamp, and a miniature model of a B-17 bomber. On the wall behind Parker were several framed photographs of aircraft in flight, a testament to his career and achievements. The faint smell of leather and polished wood filled the room, adding to the air of authority.

Parker asked me to sit in the hard-backed chair across his desk. "Gabrowski, you've shown dedication and effort," Parker began, looking me in the eye. "But your flight evaluations have consistently shown areas where you struggle. We've decided that it's in the best interest of Army Air Forces that you be reassigned."

My throat tightened. "Reassigned, sir?"

"Yes," Parker said. "You'll be transitioning to navigator training. It's an important role, and I believe you'll excel there."

I sheepishly nodded, trying to process the crushing disappointment. "Yes, sir. Thank you, sir."

Parker leaned forward, his tone softening slightly. "I know this is hard to hear, Vincent. You're not the first cadet to face this, and you won't be the last. Many of the best navigators and bombardiers started as pilot trainees. This isn't the end of your career—it's just a new direction."

With that, I walked back to the barracks in a daze. Tony was waiting for me, a broad grin on his face. "So, what did Parker say? We're moving on together, right?"

I shook my head, forcing a smile. "No, I'm being reassigned to navigator training."

Tony's smile faltered. "What? That can't be right! You've been working just as hard as I have."

"Apparently, not hard enough, but it's fine. I'll be fine."

Just as I was about to enter the barracks, Sergeant Sanders approached me. "Gabrowski, the commander wants to see you immediately."

My heart skipped as I followed Sanders to the commander's office. I couldn't imagine what more news could come my way.

The commander's office was imposing, with heavy wooden furniture and walls adorned with military memorabilia. Commander Harkins, a stern-looking man with graying hair, sat behind his desk. Little did I know my life was about to take an unexpected turn.

"Cadet Gabrowski, please sit," he said, gesturing to a chair.

I sat down, feeling the tension in the room. "Sir, is there a problem?"

Commander Harkins sighed, looking at a file on his desk. "Vincent, I have some difficult news. We received a telegram this morning. Your mother is gravely ill. The doctors don't expect her to have much time left."

The news hit me like a ton of bricks, and I struggled to keep my emotions in check.

A lump formed in my throat. "My mother...?"

Harkins nodded solemnly. "You're being granted emergency leave to go home and be with her. We have already arranged your travel."

I sat there, stunned, trying to process the news. Mom's face flashed in my mind, and the thought of losing her was overwhelming.

"Thank you, sir," I managed to say, my voice barely a whisper.

Harkins stood and walked around the desk, touching my shoulder. "Take all the time you need, Vincent. Family is important, and you must be with yours right now."

As I packed my things, Tony watched with concern. "What's going on?"

"My mom... she's dying. Tomorrow, I will start my leave and travel home to see her."

Tony's face fell. "I'm so sorry. Is there anything I can do?"

I shook my head. "Just take care of things here. I'll be back as soon as I can."

We hugged, and I could feel Tony's support and concern. "Stay strong, Vince. Your mom's lucky to have you."

That night, perhaps one of the longest in my life, I lay awake in my bunk, staring at the ceiling. I could hear the muted conversations and laughter of the other cadets, their excitement noticeable as they celebrated their progress. Tony tried to console me, but I pushed him away, needing time alone to grapple with my feelings. The dream of becoming a pilot, which I had nurtured for a long time, had slipped away, but right now, it didn't really matter. I felt a profound sense of failure and envy as I thought of Tony and the others moving on without me. The neatly framed photographs in Parker's office seemed to taunt me, reminding me that I wasn't good enough.

I felt mixed emotions as I boarded the bus to the train station. The disappointment of my reassignment was now overshadowed by the urgent need to be with my family. The journey ahead was uncertain, but I knew I had to face it with the same determination I had shown in my training, regardless of the outcome. The road to California would have to wait. For now, my place was at home with Mom, making the most of the time she had left.

CHAPTER 11

During the train ride back, a state of confusion, anger, and sadness crept over me. I sat alone, wallowing in thoughts of my dying mother, my dreams of being a bomber pilot shattered, and my future with Marya too distant to grasp. The clatter of the train on the tracks did little to soothe my troubled mind.

I tried to feign sleep, hoping to escape the turmoil in my head, but my thoughts were relentless. Images of my mother's smiling face, now etched with illness, mingled with the bitter disappointment of my reassignment and the longing for Marya.

Suddenly, I felt a hand on my shoulder. Startled, I opened my eyes and looked up to see a man in a uniform standing beside me. His face was kind, and there was a hint of understanding in his eyes.

"Mind if I sit here?" he asked gently.

I nodded, too weary to protest. He settled into the seat beside me, placing his cap on his lap. "You look like you could use someone to talk to," he said.

I sighed, not sure where to begin. "It's been a rough few days," I admitted, my voice barely above a whisper.

The man nodded. "I'm Lieutenant Colonel Harrington. Sometimes, it helps to talk about it. What's on your mind?"

I hesitated, and then the words began to spill out. "My mother is dying, and I'm on my way home to see her. I just learned I'm being reassigned from pilot training to navigator training. And Marya... well, I haven't heard from her yet."

Colonel Harrington listened patiently, his expression never wavering. "I'm sorry to hear about your mother, Vincent. That's a heavy burden to carry. And it sounds like you've been through a lot with your training."

I nodded, feeling a lump in my throat. "I wanted to be a pilot more than anything. Now... I don't know if I can handle any more disappointment." I also silently questioned how he knew my first name.

Colonel Harrington leaned back in his seat, looking thoughtful. "I understand how you feel. My journey hasn't been easy either. But sometimes, the path we end up on isn't the one we planned, and that's okay. Every role is important, especially in times like these."

I looked at him, searching for the truth in his words. "But what if I'm not cut out for this? What if I keep failing?"

Colonel Harrington smiled gently. "Failure is a part of life, Vincent. It's what you do after you fail that defines you. From what I can fathom about you, you have the determination and the heart to overcome these setbacks. And remember, being a navigator is crucial. You'll be guiding your crew, ensuring their safety. That's no small task."

His words began to sink in, and I felt a glimmer of hope. "I guess you're right. It's just hard to see it that way right now."

Colonel Harrington nodded. "I know. But take it one day at a time. Focus on being there for your mother now. The rest will come in time."

As the train continued, I opened up more to Colonel Harrington. We talked about our families, our dreams, and the war that had turned our lives upside down. His presence comforted me, and I realized I wasn't as alone as I had felt.

When the train finally pulled into the station, he offered his hand. "Take care of yourself, Vincent. And remember, you're stronger than you think."

I shook his hand, feeling a surge of gratitude. "Thank you, sir. I needed that."

He nodded, then disappeared into the crowd. Little did I know that he would become my commanding officer overseas.

I took a deep breath and stepped off the train, ready to face whatever awaited me at home.

CHAPTER 12

As the train pulled into the station at Hamtramck, I felt a mixture of dread and relief. I stepped onto the platform, my heart heavy with the anticipation of seeing my mother and the sadness of knowing it would be for the last time. I looked around, scanning for any familiar faces, and then I saw her.

Marya stood there, her eyes searching through the crowd until they met mine. She looked as beautiful as ever, though concern and sadness clouded her features. She hurried towards me, and we were in each other's arms in an instant.

"Vincent," she said softly, her voice trembling with emotion, her eyes filled with tears.

"Marya, I am so glad you're here," I replied, holding her tightly.

We walked together through the familiar streets of my hometown, memories flooding back with each step. The smell of fresh bread, children playing in the park, and the sound of church bells in the distance reminded me of simpler times.

"How is she?" Marya asked, her voice filled with concern.

I sighed, feeling the weight of the world on my shoulders. "Not good. They don't think she has much time left."

We reached my house; my heart began beating heavier. The door creaked open, and there Mom was, frail and lying in a bed set up in the living room. Her eyes lit up when she saw me, and she reached out a trembling hand.

"Wincenty," she whispered, a smile spreading across her face.

I rushed to her side, tears streaming down my face. "Mom, I'm here."

Marya stood by, giving us a moment before greeting my mother warmly. "Hello, Mrs. Gabrowski."

Mom smiled at Marya. "Marya, it's good to see you. Thank you for being here."

We spent the next few days together, sharing stories, laughter, and tears. Mom's strength and grace in her final days were a testament to her character.

As the sun set a warm glow across her room one evening, Mom called me to her side.

"Wincenty," she began softly, her voice a gentle whisper, "come sit with me."

I moved closer, taking her frail hand in mine.

She looked at me with eyes filled with a lifetime of love and wisdom. "I remember when you were just a little boy, always curious and full of dreams. You've grown into such a strong, courageous man. I'm so proud of you."

I swallowed hard, trying to control my emotions. "Thank you, Mom. You've always been my inspiration."

Marya, who had been quietly sitting nearby, came over and touched my shoulder. Mom smiled at her.

"Marya," she said, her voice a bit stronger, "you've been a blessing to Wincenty. Thank you for being here for him."

"It's my honor, Mrs. Gabrowski," Marya replied, tears welling in her eyes. "Vincent means everything to me."

Mom nodded, her eyes twinkling with a hint of mischief. "I always knew you two were meant for each other. Promise me you'll take care of each other."

"We promise," Marya and I said in unison, our voices filled with conviction.

As the night grew darker, Mom and I continued to talk. She shared stories from her youth, tales of resilience and hope, reminding me of the strength she had always possessed.

"Mom, do you remember when you used to bake those apple pies every Sunday?" I asked, a smile spreading across my face at the memory.

She chuckled softly. "Of course I do. You and your sisters would hover around the kitchen, waiting for a slice."

"I can still smell them," I said, feeling nostalgic. "Those are some of my best memories."

We sat in comfortable silence for a while, the only sound the gentle rustle of the curtains in the evening breeze. Finally, she spoke again, her voice filled with a serene calm.

"Wincenty, life is full of challenges. But it's also full of beauty and love. Never lose sight of that. Promise me you'll keep fighting, no matter what."

I leaned down, kissing her forehead. "I promise, Mom. I promise."

She told me how proud she was of me, no matter what path I chose.

She passed away peacefully that night, and though my heart ached, I felt a sense of peace. I could say goodbye, share those precious moments, and have Marya by my side.

The visitation for Sophia Grabowski, née Smyleski, lasted two days, and at her funeral mass, a large crowd attended. I sat in the pew next to my Dad while Marya and I comforted my three sisters, all in tears and wanting to stay close to me. At that moment, I desperately wanted to stay home, marry Marya, and support Dad and my sisters. However, I knew that my new home would be in California in a few days.

CHAPTER 13

The long bus ride from Maxwell Field to Mather Field in California felt like a journey into the unknown. As the bus rumbled through the changing landscapes of America, I couldn't help but reflect on the twists and turns my life had taken. The disappointment of washing out of pilot training still lingered, but I was resolute, determined to embrace my new role as a navigator-in-training.

Reassigned cadets packed the bus, each carrying our burdens of disappointment and hope. I sat beside Stenson Falwell, a tall, lanky cadet with a serious demeanor. He looked as lost in thought as I felt, staring out the window as the scenery changed from flat plains to rolling hills. In that moment, we were all united in our shared journey, shared dreams, and shared determination to make the best of our new roles.

"Hey," I said, trying to strike up a conversation. "I'm Vincent Gabrowski. Everyone calls me Vince."

Stenson turned to me and offered a small smile. "Stenson Falwell. Nice to meet you, Vince."

"You heading to Mather Field for navigator training too?" I asked.

"Yeah," Stenson replied, his voice tinged with resignation and determination. "I washed out of pilot training back at Maxwell. Guess we're in the same boat."

I nodded. "Same here. It's tough, but I'm trying to see it as a new opportunity."

Stenson sighed. "I know what you mean. I've wanted to be a pilot for as long as I can remember. My old man was a pilot in the Great War, and I wanted to follow in his footsteps. Guess it wasn't meant to be."

As the bus continued its journey, Stenson and I shared our stories. He told me about his family back in Kansas, their small farm, and his father's stories of flying over the trenches in the First World War. I told him about my family in Michigan, my dreams of soaring through the skies, and the camaraderie I had found with Tony and the other cadets.

"Funny how life turns out," Stenson mused. "One moment you're dreaming of flying, the next you're on a bus to learn how to navigate instead."

"Yeah," I agreed. "But at least we're still part of the effort. Being a navigator is important, too. We're making sure those pilots get where they need to go."

Stenson nodded thoughtfully. "You're right. My dad always said that every role in the military is crucial. It's hard to let go of the dream, you know?"

"I get it," I said, my voice filled with optimism. "But maybe this is just a different kind of adventure. A new way to make a difference, a new path to explore."

The bus ride stretched on, with hours turning into days. We traveled through bustling cities and quiet towns across endless fields and towering mountains. The further west we went, the more the landscape changed, becoming more rugged and dramatic.

"California's supposed to be beautiful," Stenson said one afternoon as we drove past a particularly stunning vista in Arizona. "Have you ever been there?"

I shook my head. "Nope, it's the first time for me. I've heard great things, though."

"Yeah, me too," Stenson replied. "Maybe this won't be so bad after all."

As we neared Mather Field, the mood on the bus began to shift. The initial disappointment and apprehension gave way to anticipation. We were all about to embark on a new chapter, one that would still allow us to contribute meaningfully to the war effort.

"We're almost there," I said, looking out the window as the outskirts of Sacramento came into view.

Stenson smiled. "New beginnings, right?"

"Right," I agreed. "New beginnings."

When the bus finally pulled into Mather Field, the sight of aircraft and bustling activity greeted us; the air filled with the hum of engines and the shouts of instructors. It was a new world, but one that felt strangely familiar.

As we stepped off the bus, an officer approached us. "Welcome to Mather Field, gentlemen. Fall in line and prepare for your new assignments."

I looked at Stenson and smiled. "Here we go."

He grinned back. "Let's make the most of it, Vince."

With that, we joined the line of new arrivals, ready to face the challenges ahead. The journey had been long, but it was just the beginning of a new adventure that would test our skills, resolve, and determination to serve our country.

As we settled into our new surroundings, I felt a renewed sense of purpose. The path to becoming a pilot had ended, but a new path had opened up, one that held its own promise and potential. With new friends like Stenson by my side, I knew I could face whatever came next.

CHAPTER 14

The first day of navigator training at Mather Field was a whirlwind of introductions, instructions, and new routines. Stenson, I, and the other cadets, united in our shared mission, were gathered in a large lecture hall. Maps and charts adorned the walls, and the air buzzed nervously.

Our training officer, Captain Davis, stood at the front of the room. He was a tall man with a stern expression, but his eyes held a hint of encouragement. "Welcome to navigator training, gentlemen," he began. "You are here because you have shown the potential to excel in one of the most critical roles in the Army Air Forces. The success of every mission relies heavily on your skills and accuracy."

He paused, giving time to let his words sink in. "Over the next several weeks, each one of you cadets will be challenged in ways you haven't been before. You will learn to navigate using celestial bodies, dead reckoning, and radio signals. You'll master using charts, compasses, and various navigation instruments. When you leave here, you can guide your crew safely to any destination, day or night, in any weather."

Intensive classroom instruction filled the days. We spent hours learning about the principles of navigation, the layout of aeronautical charts, and the use of different navigation tools. The complexity of the subject matter often left us scratching our heads.

Captain Davis, pointing to a large chart on the wall, said, "This is your new best friend, gentlemen. An aeronautical chart shows you everything you need to know about the terrain, airspace, and navigational aids in a given area. Learn to read it like you would a book."

Stenson leaned over to me, whispering, "This is like trying to learn a new language."

I nodded, feeling equally overwhelmed. "We just have to take it one step at a time," I said, my determination to excel in this critical role unwavering.

Practical exercises quickly supplemented our classroom learning. We were given charts and tasked with plotting courses, calculating distances, and estimating arrival times.

One afternoon, Captain Davis handed us a set of coordinates. "You have two hours to plot a course from here to our training site in the Sierra Nevada Mountain Range. Remember to account for wind speed and direction. Good luck."

Stenson and I huddled over our charts, furrowing our brows in concentration. "Okay, we start here," I said, pointing to Mather Field. "We need to head northeast."

"Got it," Stenson replied, marking the course on his chart. "But don't forget the wind correction angle."

I calculated quickly. "We need to adjust five degrees to the east."

After plotting our course, we handed our charts to Captain Davis. He scrutinized them, then gave a curt nod. "Good work, Gabbro, Falwell. You're getting the hang of it. Oh, by the way, Gabrowski, I've shortened your name."

"Thank you, sir," I responded.

Night navigation was a different beast altogether. The instructors taught us to use celestial bodies—stars, planets, and the moon—to find our way.

One clear evening, we gathered outside with our sextants, which are used to measure the angle between a celestial body and the horizon. Captain Davis pointed to the sky. "The North Star, or Polaris, is your most reliable guide at night. It's almost directly over the North Pole, and its position doesn't change."

We took turns using the sextant, trying to get accurate readings. It was challenging, but the breathtaking beauty of the night sky, with its myriad of stars, made the task feel almost magical.

Stenson struggled with his sextant, squinting at the stars. "How do you even know which one is Polaris?" he muttered.

I pointed it out. "Look for the Big Dipper. The two stars at the end of the bowl point right to it."

"I got it," Stenson said, adjusting his sextant. "This is harder than it looks."

As our training progressed, we moved on to flight simulations. These simulations took place in large rooms with mock-up aircraft cabins. We practiced our skills in a controlled environment, learning to make quick decisions and adjustments based on simulated flight conditions.

One day, Captain Davis announced, "Today, we'll be simulating a mission over the Pacific. You'll have to navigate using both dead reckoning and celestial navigation. Remember, your accuracy is crucial."

Stenson and I worked together in the simulator, plotting our course and making constant adjustments. The pressure was intense, with the knowledge that any mistake could lead to a simulated disaster. But the experience was invaluable, teaching us to make quick decisions and adjustments based on simulated flight conditions.

"The wind's shifting again," Stenson noted, marking a change on his chart. "We need to adjust our heading."

"I got it," I replied, recalculating our course. "We should be on target now."

Despite my best efforts, I increasingly struggled with the complexities of navigation. The calculations, constant adjustments, and pressure to be precise began weighing heavily on me. I could see concern in Captain Davis's eyes as he reviewed my work, and the fear of not meeting the standards was a constant companion.

One afternoon, after another frustrating session, Captain Davis pulled me aside. "Gabbro, I can see you're putting in the effort, but your accuracy is off. We need navigators who can make split-second decisions with precision. If this continues, we'll have to consider other options for you."

My heart sank. I knew what that meant. I redoubled my efforts, spending every spare moment studying and practicing, but the results were inconsistent. My confidence began to waver, and the pressure mounted, making it harder to focus on the tasks ahead.

The culmination of our training was a final evaluation flight. We would be navigating a real aircraft, testing our skills in a high-stakes environment. It was my last chance to prove myself. On the day of the final flight, my nerves ran high. Stenson and I boarded the aircraft, feeling the weight of the moment. Captain Davis was there to oversee the mission.

As we took off, I focused on the charts before me, plotting our course precisely. Stenson handled the radio and monitored our position.

Captain Davis reminded us, "Remember to account for drift. Stay on top of your calculations."

Hours passed as we navigated through various checkpoints, adjusting as needed. I struggled to keep up with the demands, feeling the pressure of every decision. When we finally landed back at Mather Field, I knew my performance had not been up to par.

Captain Davis gathered us together. "You've done well,

gentlemen. You've proven you have what it takes to be a navigator. However, some of you have shown greater aptitude than others."

He turned to me with a serious but kind expression. "Gabbro, I'm sorry, but your accuracy and decision-making have not met the necessary standards for a navigator. We'll need to discuss your reassignment in my office."

My throat tightened, and I nodded, unable to find the words. The disappointment was crushing, but I knew I had to face it. The walk to Captain Davis's office felt like a mile instead of a few yards. When I sat down, Captain Davis looked at me with a mixture of empathy and resolve. "Vincent, I can see how hard you've been working, and your dedication is commendable. However, your navigation evaluations indicate some persistent challenges we can't overlook. We've decided to reassign you."

A knot formed in my stomach. "Reassigned, sir?"

Davis nodded solemnly. "Yes, Vincent. You are better suited for gunnery training. It's a critical role, and I have confidence in your ability, strength, and stamina to excel as a gunner."

I struggled to absorb the news, feeling a wave of disappointment. "I understand, sir. Thank you."

Leaning forward, Davis spoke more softly. "Vincent, this isn't a failure. Many exceptional gunners began their journeys in different roles. This reassignment isn't the end of your career; it's a new opportunity to contribute significantly. You have the resilience and the skill set needed to protect your crew from one of the most crucial positions on the plane."

I nodded again, more securely this time. "I appreciate the opportunity, sir. I'll give it my best."

"Good," Davis said with a firm nod. "I'm confident you will."

With that, I left Davis's office, and I was determined to face this new challenge head-on.

CHAPTER 15

The bus ride to the Las Vegas Army Airfield in Nevada felt like a walk in the park compared to the long bus drive from Maxwell Field to Mather Field. I now made it a point to focus on becoming the best gunner in the Army Air Forces. The landscape changed from the green fields and trees of California to the arid desert, with its endless stretches of sand and rock. The sun blazed overhead, and the heat seeped through the bus windows, but I barely noticed; my mind was set on the new challenges ahead.

As we pulled into the airfield, the vastness of the base struck me. It was a sprawling complex with rows of barracks, training facilities, and, of course, the planes. The constant roar of engines, the sight of bombers lined up in perfect formation, and the sound of gunfire filled me with a renewed sense of purpose. I stepped off the bus, my duffel bag slung over my shoulder, and took in my surroundings. The air was dry and hot, starkly contrasting the cool mornings I had grown accustomed to in California. But the change of scenery was invigorating. I was ready to tackle whatever came my way.

"Welcome to Las Vegas Army Airfield, gentlemen!" barked a grizzled sergeant, his voice cutting through the noise. "I'm Sergeant Peterson, and I'll oversee your gunnery training. From now on, you eat, sleep, and breathe this base. Understood?"

"Yes, sir!" we replied in unison, our voices strong and determined.

We ran to our new barracks, simple yet functional, where

we quickly stowed our gear. The camaraderie among the cadets was immediate; every one of us focused on not washing out from gunnery school. We certainly didn't want to be assigned to ground crew positions, administrative duties, or other support roles. After eating in the mess hall that evening, I stood outside, looking at the clear desert sky. The stars were incredibly bright, undimmed by city lights, and I felt a strange sense of peace. Despite the disappointments and the hardships, I was exactly where I needed to be.

The following day, training began in earnest. Sergeant Peterson wasted no time putting us through our paces. We started with the basics: handling and maintaining the fifty-caliber machine guns that would be our lifeline in the air.

"These guns are your best friends up there," Peterson explained, his voice booming across the training field. "You need to know them inside and out. Take them apart, put them back together, and make sure they're clean and functioning. Your life depends on it. Also, be sure to remember that you fire in controlled bursts for accuracy and so that your gun barrels don't overheat."

We spent hours in the scorching sun, learning every component of the machine guns, practicing loading and unloading, and honing our aim on the firing range. Gunfire echoed through the air, a constant reminder of the reality we would soon face.

During a break, I spoke with a fellow cadet named Benny Soslowski. He was a short, stocky guy with a perpetual smile. Still, his eyes held a seriousness that belied his casual demeanor.

"Hey, Vince," he said, wiping sweat from his brow. "How'd you end up here?"

I shrugged, taking a swig of water. "Washed out of pilot training. I then tried navigating, but that didn't pan out either. I guess I'll be a gunner."

Soslowski nodded. "Same here. I tried to be a pilot, but it wasn't in the cards. It's tough, but at least we're still in the fight."

"Yeah," I agreed. "At least we're still part of the team."

As the weeks went by, the training intensified. We practiced in mock-up turrets, simulating the cramped, dizzying conditions we would face in combat. The instructors taught us the importance of teamwork and communication, essential skills for surviving in the chaos of aerial warfare.

"Keep your eyes peeled and your ears open," Peterson would remind us. "Your job is to protect the plane and your crewmates. One mistake could cost lives!"

The physical and mental demands were relentless, but I felt myself growing stronger and more focused. Each day, I was a step closer to becoming the gunner I needed to be. One evening, after a particularly grueling training day, I received a letter from Marya. Her words were a balm to my weary soul, filled with love and encouragement. She wrote about life back home, how she kept busy and stayed strong, and how much she missed me.

"Honey," she wrote, "I know you'll be an amazing gunner. You've always had a strong heart and a brave spirit. Remember that I'm here, waiting for you, and our love will see us through this. Stay safe, my love."

Her words renewed my determination. I would become the best gunner I could be, not just for myself but also for Marya, Mom, and everyone who believed in me.

As the final weeks of training approached, the intensity reached its peak. We participated in live-fire exercises, shooting at moving targets from the turrets of actual bombers. The experience was both exhilarating and terrifying, a stark reminder of the reality we would soon face.

On the last day of training, Sergeant Peterson gathered us together. "You've come a long way," he said, his voice filled with pride. "You've proven yourselves capable and ready. Remember what you've learned here and carry it into the skies. Good luck and may you all come back safely. You cadets are now full-fledged gunners."

We stood at attention, our hearts swelling with pride and apprehension. As I looked around at my fellow gunners, I felt a deep sense of camaraderie. We were a team, bonded by our shared experiences and the knowledge that we would soon face the unknown together.

As we boarded the plane for our next assignment, I took one last look at the Las Vegas Army Airfield. It had been a place of transformation, where I had faced my fears and found my true calling. Whatever lay ahead, I was ready to face it head-on, with the support of my crew and the love of those waiting for me back home.

CHAPTER 16

Becoming a skilled gunner in the Army Air Forces, the AAF, was a journey of resilience, marked by challenges, setbacks, and relentless perseverance. My path was far from straightforward, yet each obstacle only served to shape me into a more resilient and capable airman, ready for the trials of combat. After successfully passing gunnery training, I earned the rank of Sergeant.

Three years had passed since I became an Aviation Cadet, and it had been two years since I earned my wings as a gunner before I set foot on the Amendola Airfield in Foggia, Italy. Between the time I became a gunner and my assignment in the 15th AAF with the 2nd Bombardment Group, 20th Bomb Squadron, my varied background made me a candidate for specialized training and temporary assignments. These roles included technical support and additional instruction, further delaying my deployment but enriching my skill set.

Deployment logistics and assignment to the 2nd Bomb Group also took time. They had me stationed at various airfields, honing my skills, preparing operationally, and filling temporary roles as needed. The waiting period, though frustrating, was essential for ensuring readiness.

Then, in early 1944, I received my final assignment to the 2nd Bomb Group. The integration period was a time of intense pre-deployment training, simulated combat missions, and crew coordination exercises. This phase was crucial for building the teamwork and trust necessary for survival in combat. We spent the final months before deployment in rigorous preparation. My unit and I participated in live-fire exercises, navigation drills, and formation flying. Delays due to operational readiness checks, aircraft maintenance, or changes in strategic priorities further extended this period but made us prepared.

Throughout this extended period, I was fortunate to have occasional leave, allowing me to spend precious time with Marya. Those moments were a sanctuary, a brief respite from the relentless pace of training and preparation. During one such leave, I met Marya at our favorite café in Hamtramck. The familiar surroundings, the aroma of fresh coffee, and the warmth of her smile provided a sense of normalcy that I desperately needed.

"It's so good to see you," she said, her eyes filled with love and concern.

"I've missed you too," I replied, taking her hand. "These breaks are what keep me going."

We spent most of our days together strolling through the parks, reminiscing, and discussing our hopes for the future. The park was our escape, where the war felt distant, and we could be together. Children laughed and played around us, and the smell of blooming flowers filled the air, adding to the sense of peace.

One afternoon, as we sat by the fountain in the town square, Marya rested her head on my shoulder. "Remember when we came here after school?" she asked, her voice soft and filled with nostalgia.

I smiled, recalling those carefree days. "Yeah, we used to dream about the future, never imagining it would bring us here."

Her unwavering support and encouragement were a source of strength for me. She understood the demands of my training and the importance of my role, constantly reminding me of the bigger picture. One evening, as we walked along the river, Marya stopped and looked at me, her expression serious. The setting sun produced a glow over the water, and a gentle breeze rustled the leaves of the trees lining the bank.

"Vincent, I know this has been incredibly tough on you," she said, her eyes locking onto mine. "But I believe in you. You're going to make an incredible difference out there."

Her words resonated deeply, reinforcing my resolve. "Thank you. Your belief in me means more than you'll ever know."

She squeezed my hand, her grip firm and reassuring. "Just promise me you'll stay safe and return to me."

"I promise," I said, my voice thick with emotion. "I'll come back to you."

When my leaves ended, saying goodbye to Marya was always heart-wrenching. Each farewell was filled with promises to write and hopes for a swift end to the war. Standing on the platform and with the train ready to depart, we held each other tightly, not wanting to let go.

"I'll be waiting for you, Vincent," she whispered, her breath warm against my ear. "Stay safe."

"I will," I promised, holding her close and inhaling the scent of her hair, trying to memorize every detail. "And I will come back to you."

The train's whistle blew, signaling our final moments together. I kissed Marya, feeling deeply filled with love, hope, and a promise of return.

CHAPTER 17

The journey to Foggia, Italy aboard a B-17 Flying Fortress was a defining moment in my military career. Brimming with anticipation for the combat that awaited us, our crew embarked on the long flight across the Atlantic and over Europe, the final step before reaching Amendola Airfield. We were fully aware that soon, we'd be in the thick of the action, and this knowledge added an intensity to our preparations.

As we boarded the B-17 at our departure point in the U.S., the sight of Colonel Harrington, now a full-bird Colonel, was shocking. His presence, however, instilled a surge of confidence in us. He piloted our flight and would become our commanding officer at Amendola, bringing everything full circle since the last time I had seen him was on the train ride back home.

"Vincent, it's good to see you again," Colonel Harrington greeted me warmly as I climbed aboard. His presence was reassuring, and his demeanor was as calm and confident as ever.

"It's good to see you too, Colonel," I said while I saluted him. "I didn't expect to be flying with you."

"Life has a funny way of bringing people back together," he said with a smile. "Let's make sure we get to Foggia in one piece."

Benny, always the one to lighten the mood, was right behind me. "Hey Vince, ready for the adventure?" he asked, his grin infectious. Our camaraderie, forged through shared experiences and a common mission, was a source of strength and comfort.

"Always," I replied, slapping him on the back. "Let's get this bird in the air."

The interior of the B-17 was cramped, with barely enough room for all the crew and our equipment. The smell of oil and metal filled the air, mingling with the faint scent of sweat and adrenaline. We took our positions, ensuring everything was secured and ready for the long journey ahead.

As we taxied down the runway, the engines roared to life, vibrating through the entire aircraft. The sound was deafening but a comforting reminder of the Flying Fortress's power and resilience.

"All right, crew, let's make this a smooth flight," Colonel Harrington's voice crackled over the intercom. "We've got a long way to go, so settle in and stay sharp."

As we lifted off the ground, the familiar sensation of takeoff washed over me. The plane climbed steadily, and soon, we were cruising at altitude, the vast expanse of the Atlantic Ocean stretching out below us. Our first stop was in Newfoundland, a necessary layover for refueling and a short rest. As we descended towards the airfield, Newfoundland's rugged coastline and dense forests came into view.

"Welcome to Gander, Newfoundland," Colonel Harrington announced as we touched down. "We'll refuel here and rest tonight before the long haul over the Atlantic."

We disembarked, stretching our legs and taking in the surroundings. The airfield was bustling with activity, planes coming and going and ground crews working tirelessly.

Benny and I took a moment to breathe in the fresh air. "Feels good to be on solid ground, even if it's just for a little while," Benny said, looking around.

"Yeah, it does," I replied, feeling the chill in the air. "Let's make the most of this break."

We headed to the mess hall, where a hot meal awaited us. The food was simple but satisfying, giving us a chance to recharge. After eating, we found a quiet spot to rest before the next leg of our journey.

The following morning, we were back in the air. The vast expanse of water below was both awe-inspiring and daunting. We kept our spirits high with lighthearted banter and shared stories.

"Remember that time in Vegas when you almost melted your machine gun?" Benny asked, laughing.

"How could I forget?" I replied, shaking my head. "I thought I was toast but backed off just in time on the pace of my firing. That was a close one. Uncle Sam wouldn't have been happy with me, and I might be on the ground instead of up here with you."

Colonel Harrington occasionally chimed in over the intercom, updating us on our progress and ensuring everything ran smoothly. His calm and authoritative voice was a steadying presence, guiding us through the endless miles of open ocean.

As we approached the coast of Europe, the landscape began to change. The blue expanse of the Atlantic gave way to green and brown patches of land, with towns and cities dotting the horizon. It was a welcome sight, signaling we were approaching our destination.

"Look at that, Vince," Benny said, pointing out the window. "We're almost there."

"Yeah, it's a beautiful sight," I agreed, excited and apprehensive. The reality of what lay ahead was starting to sink in.

The final leg of our journey took us over the Mediterranean Sea and into Italy. The rugged terrain and picturesque villages starkly contrasted the war-torn images we had seen in briefings. As we neared Foggia, the tension in the plane increased. We knew that once we landed, our mission would truly begin.

"Amendola Airfield in sight," Colonel Harrington announced. "Prepare for landing."

The descent was smooth, and relief washed over me as we touched the runway. We had made it. The crew cheered, realizing we were finally in Italy, bringing a renewed sense of purpose. As we taxied to our designated area, I looked out the window and saw the bustling activity of Amendola Airfield. Planes were being refueled and repaired, and personnel were moving about with a sense of urgency. It was clear that we were now part of something much bigger.

Colonel Harrington stopped the plane and turned to address the crew. "Welcome to Foggia, gentlemen. The War begins for you today. Let's get settled in and prepare for what's ahead. We've got a lot of work to do."

Benny and I grabbed our gear and headed towards the barracks, eager to settle in and start our new chapter. As we walked, Benny nudged me and said, "Can you believe it, Vince? We're finally here."

"Yeah, it's surreal," I replied, taking a deep breath. "We're finally here ready to face the Luftwaffe fighters and the German Army's flak."

Colonel Harrington approached us as we were about to enter the barracks. "Gabrowski, Soslowski, I hope you enjoyed the flight."

"I did, Colonel, although the takeoff from Gander seemed precarious because of the crosswinds," I said, then saluted him.

"I did, too, and I'll second Vince's comment, sir," Benny added.

As we settled into our bunks, I couldn't help but think about the journey that had brought us here. From the early days of basic training to the countless hours of preparation and the long flight across the Atlantic, every step had led us to this moment.

Benny leaned over from his bunk and said, "Hey Vince, you ever think about how far we've come?"

"All the time," I replied, smiling. "But it's only the beginning.

We've got a lot more ahead of us."

With that, I closed my eyes, ready to face the dangers that lay ahead. I knew we would survive because we were prepared, united, and determined to make a difference.

CHAPTER 18

Before our introductory briefing, Benny and I had time to wander around the airfield. The stark contrast between this new environment and the training grounds back in the States immediately struck me. The air was different, filled with a mix of the smells of machinery, the faint scent of the surrounding countryside, and the distant rumble of aircraft engines. The landscape around the airfield was rugged and somewhat barren, but it had its own beauty, with the sun casting long shadows over the uneven terrain.

The airfield was a hive of operations, with aircraft constantly taking off and landing, ground crews working tirelessly on maintenance, and personnel moving urgently. Clearly, this place was a critical part of the Allied war effort, and the intensity of the operations reflected that importance.

The runways were a flurry of movement, with bombers taxiing to their designated positions, ready for their next mission. The sight of these massive planes lined up in perfect formation was truly awe-inspiring and humbling. Each silver B-17 stood as a testament to the Allied forces' engineering prowess and sheer determination, evoking a deep sense of admiration.

Ground crews swarmed around the aircraft, performing maintenance checks, refueling, and loading bombs. Their movements were not just efficient, but also precise, a well-rehearsed ballet of men and machines. The smell of aviation fuel and oil hung heavily in the air, mingling with the earthy scent of the surrounding fields. The ground crew's uniforms, stained with grease and sweat, provided clear evidence of their relentless work, earning them a deep sense of respect.

As Benny and I walked further, we noticed the various support structures that made up the base. Quonset huts and tents served as makeshift offices and living quarters, their canvas flaps fluttering in the breeze. Trucks and jeeps rumbled along the dirt paths, ferrying supplies and personnel.

"Look at this place, Vince," Benny said, his voice filled with wonder. "It's like a small city. Hard to believe we're in the middle of a war."

"Yeah," I replied, taking in the chaos around us. "It's impressive how everything runs so smoothly."

The control tower stood tall at the heart of the airfield, a beacon of order amidst the chaos. From this vantage point, air traffic controllers coordinated the movements of the aircraft, their voices crackling over the radio as they guided pilots through takeoffs and landings. The tower was a hive of activity, with operators scanning the skies and charts, ensuring that each mission proceeded as planned. It was the nerve center of the whole operation, a place where split-second decisions could mean the difference between success and disaster.

"That control tower," I said, pointing towards it, "must be the nerve center of the whole operation. Imagine the pressure those guys are under, guiding each mission through takeoffs and landings, their voices crackling over the radio."

Benny nodded. "I wouldn't want their job. One mistake, and it could be a disaster."

Nearby, the mess hall was a hub of social activity. Airmen and ground support staff gathered here to grab a quick meal, exchange stories of their missions, and find a moment of respite from the relentless pace of their duties. The sound of laughter and camaraderie filled the air, a comforting reminder of the bonds that kept them going in the face of danger. The smell of cooking food wafted through the air, a comforting reminder of the simple pleasures of home.

"Smells like they're cooking up something good," Benny said, his stomach growling audibly. "We should check it out later."

"Definitely."

In the distance, I could see the medical tents, a stark reminder of the dangers that came with our missions.

"See those medical tents?" I said, pointing them out to Benny. "That's where the real heroes are. They save lives every day."

Benny's expression grew serious. "Yeah. It's a tough job but thank God they're here."

We stood there for a moment, both of us lost in thought, the reality of our situation sinking in. Despite the bustling activity and constant movement, a sense of purpose and determination permeated the airfield. Every person, every structure, every piece of machinery was part of a larger effort to bring us one step closer to victory. As we continued our airfield tour, the gravity of our mission and the importance of our roles became increasingly apparent. Amendola Airfield was more than just a base; it symbolized resilience, strength, and the unwavering spirit of the Allied forces.

CHAPTER 19

The morning of December 11, 1944, started early at Amendola Airfield. An officer walked through the barracks, rousing us with a firm but steady voice. "Rise and shine, men. Time to get up."

I stirred awake, rubbing the sleep from my eyes. The familiar sound of reveille soon followed, echoing across the base. I quickly dressed and joined the rest of the crew in the mess hall for breakfast. The tension in the air thickened as we ate in silence, each man lost in his thoughts.

By 0500 hours, we assembled outside the briefing room. Only the key personnel from each crew went inside: the pilot, co-pilot, navigator, and bombardier. The rest of us waited, nerves running high. I leaned against a wall, trying to calm my racing thoughts.

Benny stood beside me. "Do you think we're ready for this?" he asked, his voice tinged with excitement and anxiety.

"We've trained for this," I replied, though doubts echoed in my mind. "We just need to trust our training and each other."

After what felt like an eternity, Captain David Spansky, our pilot, and Lieutenant Dale Lewandowski, our co-pilot, emerged from the briefing room, their faces serious but focused. We gathered around them, eager for the details.

"Alright, listen up," Spansky began. "Today's target is an oil refinery in Vienna, Austria. It's a critical hit for the war effort. Expect heavy flak and fighter opposition."

Lewandowski added, "The Luftwaffe won't let us take this one easily. We've got to stay sharp and follow our training."

As we absorbed the information, the reality of our first mission began to sink in. We headed out to our B-17, which had yet to be christened with a name or graced with nose art. The air was cold and crisp as we climbed aboard. Benny and I took our positions at the right and left waist gun positions respectively, checking our guns and ammunition belts and ensuring everything was in order. The familiar hum of the engines warming up filled the air, a comforting reminder of the power and reliability of our aircraft.

Spansky and Lewandowski ran through their pre-flight checks, their voices a steady stream of commands and confirmations. Barry Newfland, our navigator, was already plotting our course, with his maps spread out in front of him. Tom Phendergrast, the bombardier, carefully inspected the Norden bombsight, bomb racks, and release mechanisms, and verified the bomb load. Meanwhile, Andy Phillipowski, the radio operator, checked all the radio equipment and adjusted the radio frequencies as specified in the mission plan. George Dayton, the upper turret gunner, and Al Stasiak, the lower turret gunner, settled into their positions, checking their guns and ensuring the ammunition belts were properly loaded. Finally, the tail gunner, Phil Pappas, took his place at the aircraft's rear, verifying that the tail gun mount could traverse and elevate smoothly.

"Everyone ready?" Spansky called out over the intercom.

A chorus of eight affirmations came back, and with a final check, we were ready to go. We waited on the runway until the signal for takeoff came—a green flare shot into the air. The engines roared to life, and our B-17 began to taxi down the runway. The takeoff was smooth, and soon we were climbing into the sky, the ground falling away beneath us.

As we flew towards our target, the mood was tense but focused, and everyone tested their guns. I kept my eyes on the sky, watching for any sign of German fighter planes. The intercom crackled with occasional updates from Spansky and Newfland. Still, we flew in silence, mostly; each man lost in his thoughts.

As we neared the target, the tension increased, each of us knowing that soon the German fighters would attack. It didn't take long.

"Fighters at 9 o'clock!" Dayton shouted from his position in the upper turret.

I swung my gun around, my heart pounding in my chest. I spotted the Messerschmitt's, sleek and deadly, streaking towards us. I took a deep breath and fired, the recoil jolting my entire body. The sky was filled with gunfire and the flashes of tracers as we fought to defend our plane.

"Keep them off us!" Spansky urged, his voice steady despite the chaos.

My world narrowed to the sight of the fighters, the sound of my gun, and the feel of the aircraft beneath me. I fired in controlled bursts, each burst desperately attempting to protect my crew and our mission.

The Messerschmitt's were relentless, but we held our ground. My arms ached, but I ignored the pain, my entire being focused on the task at hand.

Not long after the fighters peeled off, more trouble started as we approached the flak fields. Black puffs of smoke erupted around us, and the B-17 shook from the force of the explosions. The Germans' notorious 88-millimeter anti-aircraft guns sent deadly shells skyward, making our approach perilous.

"Flak at 12 o'clock high!" Spansky called out, his voice calm but urgent. "Everyone, stay sharp."

I gripped my gun tightly, my eyes scanning the sky. The flak was thick, and the plane rocked violently with each near miss. The noise was loud, but I forced myself to stay focused, blocking out everything but my training. The flak remained thick, and the plane continued to shake with each near miss, but we pressed on.

"Bombardier, you have the controls," Spansky said, his voice steady despite the tension in the air.

"I have the controls," Phendergrast acknowledged. He then located the target visually and through the bombsight, guided the aircraft precisely over the target, and waited to trigger the bomb release mechanism at the calculated release point.

"Bombs away in five," Phendergrast called out from the bombardier's position. "Four, three, two, one... bombs away!"

I felt the sudden lift of our plane as our bombs dropped, and I held my breath, waiting for the impact. Moments later, the ground below us lit up with explosions as the bombs found their mark.

"Direct hit!" Phendergrast shouted, his voice filled with triumph. "We got it!"

We silently cheered, our spirits lifting despite the danger still surrounding us. But there was no time to celebrate. The flak was still thick, and we knew the fighters would come back for a second round after we turned back for friendly territory.

"Get us out of here, Spansky!" Dayton urged, his voice tense.

"Hang on, everyone," Spansky replied, his hands steady on the controls. "We're heading home."

The return flight was just as harrowing as the approach. The flak and fighters continued to dog us, but we fought back with everything we had. My arms were numb firing, but I kept going, my determination unwavering. Finally, after what felt like an eternity, the flak began to thin out, and the German fighters peeled away. The air around us grew quieter, and the tension in the plane started to ease.

"Everyone okay?" Spansky called out over the intercom.

A chorus of tired but relieved voices answered him. Everyone was okay.

As we approached Amendola Airfield, the sight of the familiar landscape below filled me with a sense of relief and accomplishment. The landing was smooth, and as the plane taxied to a stop, we let out a collective sigh of relief. We had done it. We had survived our first mission.

Disembarking from the plane, Benny and I exchanged a look of shared triumph. "We did it, Vince," Benny said, his voice filled with pride. "We did it."

"Yeah, we did," I replied, a smile spreading across my face. "Let's go debrief."

We had a shot of whiskey to calm our nerves before we recounted our mission in the debriefing room, filled with exhaustion and exhilaration. We reviewed every detail, from the flak fields to the dogfights, ensuring nothing was overlooked. Colonel Harrington was there, listening intently to our report.

"You all did an excellent job today," he said, his voice filled with pride. "This mission was a success because of your bravery and skill. Well done, gentlemen."

We exchanged smiles, the weight of our accomplishment sinking in. We had faced incredible danger and come out on top. We were ready for whatever came next. As we left the debriefing room, I glanced back at the medical tents in the distance. Inside, medics and doctors worked tirelessly to treat the wounded from our mission, their dedication and skill providing a lifeline to those who had faced the horrors of combat—a sobering reminder of the cost of war.

But today, we made it through. Tomorrow, we would need to be ready to do it all over again.

CHAPTER 20

Most of us flew another 20 missions together until what was to become our final mission on March 15, 1945. Unfortunately, our navigator, Barry Newfland, had been injured a week earlier and would no longer be flying with us. Bob Senstrom, who had been shot down over Germany a month earlier but miraculously made it back to Amendola, replaced Barry.

Dark clouds covered the morning sky, thickening the air with tension and anticipation. We climbed into our B-17, now affectionately named Hometown Gal, its nose freshly painted with Marya's figure. Lost in our thoughts, we braced ourselves for the mission ahead. The familiar roar of the engines filled the air, both comforting and ominous. Captain Spansky, with his steely blue eyes focused on the task, and Lieutenant Lewandowski ran through the pre-flight checks with their usual precision.

"Ready for takeoff," Spansky's voice crackled over the intercom, steady and calm.

As we taxied down the runway, the engines roared, a deafening sound that always stirred a mix of excitement and dread. I glanced at Benny, who flashed me a quick grin.

"Ready for another round, Vince?" he shouted over the noise.

"Always," I replied, though my stomach churned with the familiar pre-mission anxiety.

The takeoff was smooth, and the runway blurred beneath us. Hometown Gal lifted off, joining the formation of bombers heading toward Germany. Our original target was the synthetic oil fields in Ruhland, a critical blow to the German's war effort. But as we climbed to our cruising altitude, a thick fog enveloped the formation, obscuring our path and forcing us to divert to the secondary target: the synthetic oil fields in Kolin, Czechoslovakia.

"Stay tight, boys. We're diverting to Kolin. Repeat, diverting to Kolin."

Navigating through the dense fog, Senstrom was a picture of concentration, his eyes darting between the maps and the instruments. The fog was a ruthless adversary, keeping us from seeing the enemy below and leaving us vulnerable. As we approached Kolin and our target, the fog began to lift, revealing a landscape scarred by war. Luckily, we faced no fighters, but then anti-aircraft fire filled the sky, exploding in a deadly dance of flak. Hometown Gal shook violently as we flew into the storm of steel and fire, the smell of cordite filling the air.

The first hit came with a jolt that rocked the entire plane. A shell exploded near the left wing, sending shrapnel tearing through the fuselage. I could hear the scream of metal and the groans of our wounded bomber as it struggled to stay airborne.

"Engine one is hit!" George Dayton's voice was tense as he relayed the damage from his position in the upper turret.

I glanced out the window to see flames licking at the outboard left engine, black smoke trailing behind us like a dark omen. Spansky fought to keep the plane steady, his hands gripping the controls with a white-knuckled determination as he veered our bomber back toward the Russian line.

"Mayday! Mayday! Bail out! Bail out!" Captain Spansky's voice crackled over the intercom, urgency underpinning every word. The alarm bell clanged loudly, cutting through the chaos inside the B-17.

I grabbed my parachute and secured it as quickly as my shaking hands allowed. Around me, the crew moved with practiced efficiency, each man heading to his assigned exit. Phendergrast, Senstrom, and Pappas probably bailed out first, given their positions in or near the nose and rear hatch, while the rest of us moved toward the side and bomb bay doors. Captain Spansky and Lieutenant Lewandowski, who would be the last two to bail out, would do so out of the nose hatch.

I looked around one last time, seeing some of my brothers' faces, each etched with fear and resolve. We had been through so much together and now faced the ultimate test. One by one, we leaped into the void, the wind tearing at our clothes and the ground rushing to meet us. The sky was a blur of flak and fire, but there was a strange, surreal calm at that moment. I pulled my ripcord, feeling the jolt as the parachute opened, slowing my descent. I floated down, the battle still raging above, the ground approaching, and the whizzing of bullets around me.

After Captain Spansky jumped, Hometown Gal, crippled and aflame, went into a death spiral. The once mighty bomber spun out of control, plummeting with a loud roar towards the ground. The sight was terrifying and tragic, ending an era for us all.

As I neared the ground, I bent my knees slightly, preparing for impact. The moment my feet touched the ground, I absorbed the shock with my legs but still felt a jarring jolt travel up them. I quickly gathered the parachute canopy so that I wouldn't be dragged along the ground. I struggled to gather my bearings, the sounds of battle still echoing in my ears. Around me, the other crew members were landing, some more gracefully than others. We were scattered but alive.

Russian soldiers quickly surrounded me, as I was sure they did to the others, their rifles and pistols trained on my chest and aimed at my head. They were allies, but their suspicion of me was clear.

We were now Russian internees, a kinder term for prisoners,

caught in the tangled web of war. Our mission had ended in flames and smoke, but our story was far from over. We had survived the skies over Kolin and faced a new battle for survival and freedom. The bond we shared as a crew, the brotherhood forged in the crucible of war, would be our strength in the coming weeks.

CHAPTER 21

In the days that followed, the Russians moved us to a house in Sagan, Germany. The house was old, its walls bearing the weight of countless winters and the stories of those who had lived there. The air inside was musty, mingled with the smell of damp wood and dust. As the door closed behind us, we found ourselves in a strange and foreign place, far from the familiar roar of engines and the camaraderie of our bomber. We were now prisoners, guarded by Russian soldiers—two women and three men.

The soldiers watched us with a mix of curiosity and suspicion. Their uniforms were worn, their faces hardened by the rigors of war. Despite the tension, there was a sense of order in their demeanor. They led us to a second-story large room where we were to be housed during our captivity. The room was sparsely furnished, with rough wooden bunks lining the walls and flickering candles providing the only light. We sat in silence, the gravity of our situation sinking in. The reality of being Russian internees, a term that sounded kinder than it felt, was beginning to take hold. The door creaked open, and one of the soldiers entered, his stern expression leaving no room for misinterpretation.

"One of your men is dead," he said in broken English, his eyes scanning our faces for a reaction. "Robert Senstrom. He did not survive."

A collective gasp escaped our lips. Bob, the newest member of our crew, had only flown his first mission with us that day.

The news hit hard, a reminder of the dangers we had faced and the fragility of life in wartime. Tom lowered his head, his hands trembling slightly. He had been the last to see Bob alive, and the weight of that memory was evident in his eyes.

The Russian soldier turned and left, leaving us to grapple with our grief and uncertainty. The minutes stretched into hours, and the silence was broken only by the occasional murmur or the creak of the floorboards.

The following day, the interrogations began. The guards escorted each one of us into our own small, dimly lit room where Russian officers awaited us. The interrogations were grueling, each session lasting for hours on end. The questions were relentless, probing every detail of our mission, backgrounds, and loyalties.

For two more days, the interrogations continued, each session leaving us more drained and uncertain of our fate. The Russian soldiers watched us closely, never taking their eyes off our movements. We spoke little, each of us lost in our thoughts, grappling with the reality of our situation and the loss of Bob. We wondered why they interrogated us so intensely, considering the Russians were our allies.

At night, as we lay on the rough wooden bunks, the flickering candles casting shadows on the walls, we found solace in our shared camaraderie. Despite the fear and uncertainty, we drew strength from each other, knowing our bond as a crew was unbreakable.

The officers separated us after the initial three days of interrogation, taking each of us again to different locations within the house for further questioning. They intensified the interrogations, which lasted another five days, probing deeper into our personal lives, thoughts, and fears with a relentless determination to break us.

After these five grueling days, we reunited in the house—the relief of being together again contrasted with our visible exhaustion. The Russian soldiers continued to watch us closely.

Two of the Russian soldiers, women named Karina and Katerina, were our main guards since they both understood and spoke English. They were friendly but somewhat aloof. Katerina, in particular, had a way of watching us that was comforting and disturbing. Her piercing blue eyes seemed to see right through us, yet the kindness in her gaze gave us a glimmer of hope.

For two weeks, we enjoyed amenities we never thought we would experience as internees. The food was better than we expected, and we were allowed some semblance of freedom within the confines of the house. We could talk, share stories, and even laugh, trying to forget the harshness of our situation, if only for a little while. Katerina and Karina still kept a close watch on us, their presence a constant reminder of our captivity. Despite their aloofness, there were moments of genuine warmth. Katerina seemed to take an interest in our stories, intently listening as we recounted tales of home and the lives we had left behind.

But the respite was short-lived. After two weeks, the interrogations resumed. Again, the guards escorted us to different locations within the house. The officers were even more relentless, their questions probing deeper into our minds and souls. The interrogations lasted seven days, each session more grueling than the last.

Since Hometown Gal went down, nearly a month had passed. For us, time stood still, or so it seemed, our days blending into each other in a relentless cycle of uncertainty and fear.

CHAPTER 22

The memory of those fifteen days of interrogation remains vivid, etched into my mind like scars in the wild blue yonder. As I sit at my desk, recounting the events that shaped our fates, I relive those grueling sessions. The days were long, the questions relentless, and the pressure unyielding. During these interrogations, I realized our captors were more than just soldiers; they were skilled psychologists, using tactics designed to probe the depths of our minds, leaving us emotionally and mentally drained.

The first three days began with a sense of foreboding. The guards led me to a small, dimly lit room in the basement. Two officers awaited me, their expressions cold and calculating. They introduced themselves curtly before launching into their questions.

"Name, rank, and serial number," one demanded.

"Vincent Gabrowski, Staff Sergeant, 38475902," I replied, my voice steady despite the knot in my stomach.

They nodded, making notes on a clipboard. The questions started simply enough—details about our mission, the aircraft, and the targets. But as the hours passed, the questions became more invasive, delving into my personal life, thoughts, and fears.

"Tell us about your family, Sergeant Gabrowski," one of the officers asked, his tone almost conversational.

I hesitated, feeling a pang of longing for my parents and siblings back home. "I grew up in a small town in Michigan. My father worked in a factory, and my mother was a homemaker. I have three younger sisters."

The officer nodded, jotting down my responses. "And what about Marya?"

The mention of Marya caught me off guard. How did they know about her? "She... she's my high school sweetheart," I stammered. "We planned to get married, but she wanted to wait until I returned."

The officer's eyes gleamed with interest. "How does it feel, knowing you might never see her again?"

The question hit like a sucker punch, but I refused to let them see my pain. "It hurts," I admitted, "but I have to focus on surviving and getting back to her."

By the end of the third day, I felt emotionally drained, every nerve in my body raw and exposed. The officers' relentless questioning had chipped away at my defenses, leaving me vulnerable and weary. Yet, I held on, refusing to let them break me.

The fourth day began with a new level of intensity. The same officers were there, but this time, Dr. Volkov, a psychologist, joined them. His presence made the room feel even smaller, his gaze piercing as he observed my every move.

"Sergeant Gabrowski let's talk about your fears," Volkov began, his voice calm and measured. "What scares you the most?"

I inhaled slowly, trying to steady my nerves. "I'm scared of losing my friends, of being unable to protect them."

Volkov leaned forward, his eyes narrowing. "And how do you cope with that fear?"

"I focus on my training, on doing my job the best I can," I replied, my voice wavering slightly.

The questions became more probing, the psychologist's tactics designed to break down my mental defenses. He delved into my childhood, my relationships, and my deepest insecurities.

On the fifth day, the physical strain I felt added to the psychological assault. They kept the room cold, the discomfort adding to the mental strain, making it clear that they were using every means to break us.

"Sergeant Gabrowski, how do you handle the pressure of combat?" one of the officers asked.

"I rely on my training and my crew," I answered, shivering from the cold.

Volkov chimed in. "Do you ever doubt your abilities?"

I shook my head, trying to hide my exhaustion. "I can't afford to doubt myself. My crew depends on me."

They pushed harder, their questions designed to exploit any weakness. They asked about my nightmares, my regrets, and my fears for the future. By the end of the fifth day, I felt like a hollow shell; my mind and body stretched to their limits.

On the sixth and seventh days, they brought personal attacks. The officers seemed intent on breaking me down by attacking my sense of self-worth, their words like daggers aimed at my resolve.

"Sergeant Gabrowski, do you think you're a good airman?" one of the officers asked, his tone almost mocking.

"I do my best," I replied, my voice barely above a whisper.

Volkov leaned in, his eyes cold and calculating. "But is your best good enough? You've seen your friends die; you've been captured. Do you think you've failed?"

The question struck a nerve, but I refused to let them see my pain. "I've done everything I can to protect my crew," I said, my voice more robust than I felt.

They continued to press, questioning my decisions, leadership, and worth as an airman. Each question blew my psyche, chipping away at my resolve. But I held on, drawing strength from the memories of my brothers and the bond we shared.

By the eighth day, I was emotionally and physically exhausted, every fiber of my mind and body worn down by the relentless interrogation.

The ninth day began with a new tactic: isolation. They left me alone in the cold, dark room for hours, the silence broken only by the occasional sound of footsteps outside the door. The isolation was debilitating, the lack of human contact amplifying my fears and doubts.

When they finally returned, their questions were more intense, their tactics more ruthless. The psychologist relished my discomfort, his questions probing deeper into my psyche.

"Sergeant Gabrowski, do you ever think about giving up?" he asked, his voice whispering in the darkness.

"No," I replied, my voice firm despite my exhaustion. "I'll never give up."

Dr. Volkov's eyes gleamed with a predatory satisfaction. "We'll see about that."

The tenth and eleventh days brought false promises of comfort and safety. Instead of threats and pressure, they offered temptations of relief.

"Sergeant Gabrowski, if you cooperate, we can make things easier for you," one of the officers said, his voice smooth and persuasive.

I knew better than to trust them, but the promise of relief was tempting. "What do you want from me?" I asked, my voice tinged with desperation.

"Just tell us what we want to know," Volkov said, his tone almost gentle. "We'll take care of you."

I shook my head, the weariness in my body matched by the resolve in my heart. "I've answered all of your questions. I don't know what you want!"

Their disappointment showed, and they resumed their relentless questioning, their false kindness replaced by cold determination.

On the twelfth day, the interrogations became even more brutal. The officers and Volkov pushed harder than ever, their questions relentless, their tactics brutal. The physical and mental strain was overwhelming, my body and mind screaming for relief.

"Sergeant Gabrowski, this is your last chance," Volkov said, his voice low and menacing. "Tell us what we want to know or suffer the consequences."

I looked him in the eye, my resolve unbroken. "I don't know what you want," I said, my voice strong despite the exhaustion.

His eyes narrowed, and he leaned back, a cold smile on his lips. "Very well. You leave us no choice."

The final days were a blur of questions, threats, and pain. They used every tactic at their disposal, trying to break me, but I held firm.

After fifteen days of grueling interrogation, the entire crew reunited. The relief of being together again was welcomed, though we were all visibly and mentally exhausted. Katerina and Karina watched us closely, their presence a constant reminder of our captivity.

At night, as we lay on our bunks, we found solace in each other's presence. The bond we shared as a crew, the brotherhood forged in the crucible of war, would be our strength in the days to come. We were determined to survive, to find a way back home, and to honor the memory of Bob Senstrom, our fallen comrade.

CHAPTER 23

We were back together, sharing our stories, trying to piece together what had happened and what might come next. But for me, those two weeks were marked by something unexpected and profoundly confusing: Katerina.

Her piercing blue eyes seemed to soften whenever they met mine, and the warmth in her gaze contrasted sharply with the cold, rugged demeanor of the other guards. Her golden hair lay gracefully on her shoulders, surrounding a face of pure beauty, with lips touched by a soft rose hue. How could I think that way when I was in love with Marya? Did the interrogations do something to me? The internal turmoil I felt threatened to upend the love I held for Marya.

One evening, Katerina approached me. "Vincent," she said softly, her accent thick but her English clear. "You look tired. Come with me."

I followed her through the dimly lit hallways of the house, my heart pounding in my chest. She led me to a small bathroom with a tub filled with steaming water. "I thought you might like a bath," she said, her voice almost shy.

"Thank you, Katerina," I replied, my voice barely above a whisper. The gesture was kind, almost intimate, and it left me feeling more vulnerable than during the interrogations.

As I sank into the warm water, I closed my eyes, letting the heat soothe my aching muscles. The door creaked open, and

Katerina stepped inside, carrying a towel. She sat on a stool next to the tub, her eyes never leaving mine.

"You must be wondering why I'm doing this," she said, her voice barely audible over the sound of the running water.

"I am," I admitted, my curiosity piqued. "Why me? Why not Captain Spansky or one of the others?"

Katerina hesitated, her eyes searching mine for a moment before she spoke. "There is something about you, Vincent. You have a strength, a resilience that I admire. And... I feel a connection with you, something I can't explain."

Her words sent a shiver down my spine. I felt the same inexplicable pull towards her, tinged with suspicion. Was this a genuine connection, or was it some ploy?

Over the next few days, Katerina's attention became more frequent and more personal. She brought me extra food, sat with me during our breaks, and even shared stories of her life before the war. I learned that she had joined the army to protect her parents after the Germans destroyed her grandparents' village, a common tactic of the German military and part of their scorched earth policy.

One evening, as we sat together in the small garden behind the house, Katerina opened up to me. "I have seen so much pain and suffering, Vincent," she said, trembling. "I don't want to lose myself in this war. You remind me of what it means to be human."

Her vulnerability touched me deeply, and I found myself reaching out to take her hand despite feeling I was betraying Marya. "Katerina, I feel the same way. You are a reminder that there is still kindness and hope in this world."

Our hands lingered together, the warmth of her touch spreading through me. Our bond grew more substantial as the days passed, and my connection to Marya grew weaker. We would steal moments together, away from the watchful eyes of the other guards. There was a magnetic pull between us, an attraction we could neither deny nor control.

One night, as we sat in the kitchen after the others had gone to bed, Katerina leaned in close, her breath warm against my ear. "Vincent, I need to tell you something," she whispered. "I have been ordered to watch you closely."

I pulled back, my heart racing. "Why? Why me?"

"I don't know," she admitted, her eyes filled with genuine confusion and fear. "But I had to tell you. I don't want to lie to you."

Her honesty was both a relief and a cause for concern. "What should we do?" I asked, my mind racing with possibilities.

"We must be careful," she said, her voice urgent. "They are watching us, but I will do everything I can to protect you."

In the days that followed, our relationship deepened, each moment charged with a mix of passion and danger. We would steal kisses in the shadows, our hearts pounding with the fear of being caught. The danger of our love was a constant companion, adding a thrilling yet terrifying edge to our stolen moments. But despite the growing suspicion and the ever-present danger, we couldn't stay away from each other. Each touch, each whispered word, felt like a lifeline, a reminder that there was still something worth fighting for in this bleak, war-torn world.

The more time I spent with Katerina, the more my crew began to notice the change in our dynamic. One afternoon, as we sat in the common room, George leaned in close, his voice barely a whisper. "Vince, what's going on with you and Katerina?"

I glanced around to make sure no one else was listening. "We're... we're just talking, George. Nothing more."

"Doesn't look like nothing more," George replied, his eyes narrowing. "Be careful, Vince. The others are starting to talk too. They think something's up."

I nodded, understanding his concern. "I know, George. I'm being careful."

Despite my reassurances, the crew's suspicion grew. Phil approached me one evening, his expression serious. "Vince, I've been noticing things. Katerina spends a lot of time with you. Why?"

I sighed, running a hand through my hair. "I don't know, Phil. She says she feels a connection with me. But I'm starting to wonder if there's more to it."

Phil's eyes widened. "Like what?"

"Like she's been ordered to watch me closely," I admitted. "She told me herself. It doesn't sit right with me."

Phil frowned, his concern evident. "Just be careful. We're in enemy territory. We can't afford any mistakes."

One night, as I lay in bed, the door to our room creaked open, and Katerina slipped inside. She moved silently, eyes darting around to ensure no one saw us. She sat on the edge of my bunk, her expression tense.

"Vincent, I need to tell you something," she whispered, her voice trembling. "I overheard the officers talking. They mentioned your name, and they're planning something."

My heart raced. "What are the officers planning?"

"I don't know the details," she admitted, her eyes filled with fear. "But I think they're trying to break you, to get you to reveal something."

I took her hand, squeezing it gently. "Thank you for telling me, Katerina. I'll be careful."

As she leaned in to kiss me, the door creaked again, and Karina appeared, her eyes narrowing at the sight of us. "Katerina, you need to be more discreet," she hissed. "If they catch both of you, it'll be more trouble for Vincent, and even worse for you."

Katerina quickly stood up, her face flushed with embarrassment. "I'm sorry, Karina. I just needed to warn him."

Karina shook her head, her expression softening slightly. "I understand. But you both need to be careful. The officers are watching closely."

The tension among the crew continued to mount. Benny pulled me aside one morning, his expression serious. "Vince, we've got a problem. The other guys are talking. They're saying you're getting special treatment."

I frowned, feeling a knot of dread in my stomach. "What do you mean?"

"They're saying that Katerina has been seen with you a lot," Benny explained. "You should know that some of the crew are starting to think you're collaborating with the Russians."

"That's ridiculous," I snapped. "I'm not collaborating with anyone. She's been kind to me, that's all."

Benny's eyes softened, but his concern remained. "I believe you, Vince. But you need to be careful."

I nodded, understanding the gravity of his words. "I'll be more careful, Benny. I promise."

Despite our best efforts, the suspicion and tension continued to grow. One evening, as the crew sat together in the common room, Captain Spansky addressed us, his expression grave.

"Men, we've got a situation," he began, his voice steady. "I've heard rumblings that some of you suspect Gunner of collaborating with the Russians. I don't believe it for a second, but we must be careful. We're all in this together and need to stay united."

Captain Spansky looked directly at me, his eyes filled with concern and determination. "Vincent, I know you've been spending a lot of time with Katerina. I understand the connection you feel, but we need to be cautious. We can't afford to give anyone here reason to doubt our loyalty to each other and to the United States."

I nodded, feeling the weight of his words. "I understand, Captain. I'll be more careful. My loyalty is to the United States and to each of you."

One day, Karina approached me, her eyes narrowed with suspicion. "Vincent, be careful," she warned. "Some would use your relationship with Katerina against you."

I nodded, "Thank you, Karina. I will."

Despite the growing danger and Captain Spansky's warning, Katerina and I couldn't stay away from each other. Our connection was too strong, and our need for each other was too great. We found solace in each other's arms, a brief respite from the horrors of war. Meanwhile, my connection with Marya weakened even further.

But as the two weeks ended, I couldn't shake the feeling that something was amiss. Why had they chosen me, of all people, to be the focus of Katerina's attention? What was the true purpose behind their orders? The questions gnawed at me, even as I held Katerina close, our hearts beating in sync. There was a sense of impending doom, a fear that the harsh realities of war would shatter our fragile happiness. And yet, despite the uncertainty and the danger, I couldn't help but cling to the hope that, somehow, we would find a way to be together.

CHAPTER 24

The days following our two-week respite were heavy with a sense of impending doom. The fleeting moments of peace and connection with Katerina became a distant memory when the guards took me for another round of interrogations. This time, I faced the officers, Dr. Volkov and later his colleague, Dr. Petrov. The following five days would test the mental and physical limits of my endurance.

The familiar chill of the interrogation room seeped into my bones. Dr. Volkov, the lead psychologist, greeted me with a cold smile.

"Welcome back, Sergeant Gabrowski," he said, his voice smooth and calculating. "I trust you enjoyed your break."

I nodded, trying to hide my unease. "Yes, sir."

Dr. Volkov leaned forward, his eyes boring into mine. "Let's continue where we left off. Tell me, Sergeant, how have you been feeling?"

"Fine," I replied, keeping my answers short and guarded.

He smiled, clearly not convinced. "We noticed you spend a lot of time with Katerina. She seems quite taken with you."

I felt a surge of fear. "We're just friends," I managed to say, my voice trembling slightly.

"Are you sure Katerina and you are just friends?" he asked, drawing out the word "friends". "Tell me, Vincent, what do you feel for her?"

I hesitated, torn between loyalty and self-preservation. "I care about Katerina," I admitted, my voice betraying my inner turmoil. "But I know this isn't the place for... feelings."

Dr. Volkov nodded, making notes on his clipboard. "Interesting. Let's explore that further."

The second day began with more personal questions. Dr. Volkov seemed intent on delving deeper into my psyche, probing for weakness or vulnerability.

"Vincent, tell me about your childhood," he began, his voice almost soothing.

I recounted my memories of growing up in Michigan, my family, and my dreams of becoming a pilot. As I spoke, I noticed Dr. Volkov watching me intently, his eyes never leaving mine.

"And what about Marya?" he asked, his tone gentle. "Tell me more about her."

"Marya is my high school sweetheart," I replied, my voice tinged with sadness. "We planned to get married, but she wanted to wait until I returned."

"Do you think you'll see her again?" he pressed.

"I hope so," I said, my voice wavering.

Dr. Volkov smiled, but there was no warmth in it. "Hope is a powerful thing, Vincent. But sometimes, it's also a weakness."

"What would you tell Marya about Katerina?"

I hesitated, the weight of the question settling heavily on my shoulders. "I... I don't know," I admitted. "Marya has been a part of my life for so long. But things have changed. Katerina and I have bonded. The connection we have is... different. Intense."

Dr. Volkov nodded, his eyes studying me closely. "Does this mean you no longer love Marya?"

I looked down, my heart aching with the conflicting emotions. "I don't know if it's that simple. I care about Marya deeply, but my feelings for her have changed. Being with

Katerina is like nothing I've ever experienced before. It feels real and raw."

"And how does Katerina feel about you?" Dr. Volkov asked, his tone probing yet strangely understanding.

"She feels the same," I said softly, recalling the moments we shared, the unspoken bond that had grown between us. "We've found something in each other that we both needed. Comfort, understanding, compassion, maybe even love."

Dr. Volkov leaned back, his expression thoughtful. "Love can be a complicated and painful thing, Vincent. It often forces us to make difficult choices. Can you be honest with Marya about your feelings for Katerina?"

The thought of that conversation made my chest tighten. "I owe Marya the truth," I admitted. "But I don't know how to tell her. I don't want to hurt her."

"Hurt is inevitable in matters of the heart," Dr. Volkov said, his voice gentle but firm. "But honesty is the foundation of any meaningful relationship. You must find a way to reconcile your feelings and be true to yourself and those you care about."

On the third day, the atmosphere in the room changed. Dr. Petrov joined Volkov. Dr. Petrov specialized in hypnosis. I felt a knot form in my stomach as they explained their intention to use hypnosis as part of the interrogation.

"We believe hypnosis can help you recall details you might have forgotten," Dr. Petrov said calmly and reassuringly. "It will also help you relax."

I had no choice but to comply. Dr. Petrov's voice lulled me into trance, memories flooding back as if watching from a distance.

"Vincent, can you hear me?" Dr. Petrov's voice echoed in my mind.

"Yes," I replied, my voice distant.

"Good. I want you to go back to the day you were shot down.

What do you see?"

I described the events leading up to our crash, the flak, the fire, and the bail-out order. The memories flowed freely, unfiltered by fear or hesitation.

"And what about Katerina?" Dr. Petrov asked, his voice softer. "How do you feel about her?"

"I care about her," I said, my voice tinged with emotion. "But I don't trust my feelings."

On the fourth day, the hypnosis sessions continued. Dr. Petrov and Dr. Volkov worked together, their questions becoming more probing and manipulative.

"Vincent, do you trust your crew?" Dr. Petrov asked as I lay in a trance.

"Yes," I replied, my voice steady.

"But what if one of them is a traitor?" Dr. Volkov interjected. "What if someone has been feeding information to the Germans?"

The suggestion sent a jolt of fear through me. "No, that's not possible," I protested weakly.

"Think, Vincent," Dr. Volkov pressed. "Have you noticed anything strange about your crew? Any unusual behavior from anyone?"

The seed of doubt in my mind grew despite my attempts to resist it. "No... I don't know."

"That's good, Vincent," Dr. Petrov said soothingly. "We need you to stay vigilant. Keep an eye on your crew."

The fifth day was the most intense. The officers and two psychologists pushed harder, their questions relentless. The hypnosis sessions left me feeling disoriented and confused, my mind a whirl of doubt and suspicion.

"Vincent, you must understand," Dr. Volkov said, almost pleading. "We are trying to help you. There is a traitor among your crew, and you need find out who it is for your sake."

"No, I won't believe it," I said, my voice shaking. "What do you mean for my sake. Isn't it for your sake?"

"Think of Marya," Dr. Petrov whispered. "Think of Katerina. Don't you want to protect them?"

The manipulation was ruthless, and I felt myself breaking under the pressure. "What do you want from me?" I cried, my voice filled with desperation.

"Just the truth, Vincent," Dr. Volkov said, his eyes cold. "Tell us who the traitor is."

"I don't know!" I shouted, tears streaming down my face.

Dr. Petrov leaned in close, his voice a hiss in my ear. "You must find the traitor, Vincent. Your life, and the lives of your loved ones, depend on it."

By the end of the five days, I was a wreck. The constant questioning, the hypnosis, and the manipulation had left me broken and confused. I felt a deep sense of unease when I was finally released back to my crew. The seeds of doubt planted in my mind tainted the bond we shared.

Katerina approached me, her eyes filled with concern. "Vincent, are you okay?"

I shook my head, unable to find the words. "I don't know, Katerina. I don't know what's real anymore."

She took my hand, her touch warm and reassuring. "We'll get through this, Vincent. I promise."

But as I looked into her eyes, I couldn't shake the feeling that something was wrong. The interrogations had changed me, and the trust I once felt for my crew and Katerina was now fractured. The line between friend and foe had blurred, leaving me in perpetual suspicion.

As I lay in my bunk that night, Dr. Volkov and Dr. Petrov's words echoed in my mind. "Think of Marya. Think of Katerina.

Don't you want to protect them?"

Yes, I wanted to protect them. But at what cost? And who was I truly protecting them from?

The following days would be crucial. I had to find a way to regain my clarity, to distinguish between my captors' manipulations and the reality of my situation. The survival of my crew and my own sanity depended on it.

CHAPTER 25

A week before our release, the atmosphere in the house shifted. The guards seemed less watchful, the interrogations ceased, and there was an unspoken understanding that we were nearing the end of our captivity. The sense of impending freedom brought relief and uncertainty. One evening, as we gathered in the common room, Captain Spansky initiated a conversation that would leave a lasting impression on all of us.

"Alright, men," Spansky began, his voice steady but filled with purpose. "We've been through hell together and we're finally reaching the end of our stay here. But I want us to think about what comes next. What do you see for yourselves after the war?"

There was a moment of silence as we all pondered the question. One by one, we answered Spansky. As the conversation deepened, the intensity of our dreams and fears came to the forefront. We were no longer just airmen but visionaries, each with a unique purpose that extended beyond the battle in the air.

Spansky nodded, his expression resolute. "Then let's strengthen this pact. Let's promise to support each other in our endeavors, stay connected, and continue fighting for a better world, no matter where we end up."

We all clasped hands again, our grip firm, our eyes locked in mutual understanding and determination. In that moment, we were more than just survivors. We were a brotherhood with a mission, bound by our shared experiences and collective vision for the future. The War had tested us, but it also gave us the strength and the insight to shape a better world. We were ready to rise to that challenge together.

Or were we? Were we truly ready to shape a better world, and for whom? Despite my belief in Captain Spansky and the rest of the crew, I couldn't shake the odd feeling that as our discussion progressed, we almost seemed like automatons, merely going through the motions. The hypnosis and psychological strain we experienced left deeper marks than we realized.

CHAPTER 26

The sense of relief we had felt in the days leading up to our anticipated release was shattered when we were informed of one more day of interrogation. This time, the crew would be taken to a different location, adding to the growing tension. The uncertainty of what lay ahead weighed heavily on all of us.

That morning, we were blindfolded and led out of the house. As we were loaded into the back of a truck, our minds raced with questions and fears. The truck's engine sputtered to life, and we began a journey into the unknown. The drive lasted thirty minutes, each second stretching out interminably. The rumble of the truck and the occasional bump in the road were our only companions in the darkness of the blindfolds. Finally, the truck came to a halt, and we were roughly escorted out. The blindfolds were removed, and we found ourselves standing in front of a stark, nondescript building.

We were led inside, each of us taken to separate rooms. The rooms were small and dimly lit, the walls bare and uninviting. In each room, a team consisting of one soldier and one psychologist awaited us. The air was thick with anticipation and dread. I was seated at a metal table, facing my interrogators. The soldier, a stern-looking man with a scar across his cheek, introduced himself as Sergeant Ivanov. The psychologist, a woman with emerald green eyes and an air of quiet intensity, introduced herself as Dr. Sokolov.

"Sergeant Gabrowski," Dr. Sokolov began, her voice calm

but authoritative. "We have some final questions for you. This session will last eight hours, and we expect complete cooperation."

I nodded, trying to steady my nerves. "Yes, ma'am."

The initial questions were straightforward, almost mundane. They asked about my background, my training, and my experiences in the war. I answered each question as clearly and concisely as possible, knowing that any hesitation or inconsistency could be used against me.

"Tell us about your family," Dr. Sokolov prompted.

"I grew up in Michigan," I replied. "My father worked in the factory, and my mother took care of the home. I have three younger sisters."

"And what motivated you to join the Army Air Forces?" Sergeant Ivanov interjected.

"I wanted to become a pilot," I said, my voice steady. "I wanted to serve my country and make a difference."

As the second hour began, the questions became more probing, delving into my psyche and emotions. Dr. Sokolov's gaze seemed to pierce through me, her questions designed to uncover any hidden fears or vulnerabilities.

"Vincent, how did you cope with the stress of combat?" she asked, her tone almost clinical.

"I relied on my training and my crew," I replied. "We supported each other and worked as a team."

"But what about your personal fears?" she pressed. "Did you ever doubt yourself?"

I hesitated for a moment, then answered truthfully. "Yes, there were times I doubted myself. But I couldn't let those doubts control me. I had to stay focused for the sake of my crew."

Dr. Sokolov leaned forward, her eyes narrowing. "I am going to hypnotize you now."

My heart raced at the mention of hypnosis. I remembered the previous sessions and the unsettling feeling of losing control. But I had no choice but to comply.

Dr. Sokolov began speaking in a soothing, rhythmic voice, guiding me into a trance-like state. "Relax, Vincent. Focus on my voice. Let go of your conscious thoughts."

As I slipped into the trance, Dr. Sokolov began asking questions designed to uncover hidden memories and emotions. "Tell me about the day you were shot down. What do you remember?"

I recounted the events in vivid detail, the flak, the fire, the order to bail out. My mind was laid bare, every fear and doubt exposed.

As the fourth hour began and with the hypnotic session ended, the questions took on a more emotional tone. Dr. Sokolov and Sergeant Ivanov seemed intent on breaking me down, using my relationships and personal connections against me.

"Tell us about Marya," Dr. Sokolov said softly. "What did she mean to you?"

"She was my high school sweetheart," I replied, my voice filled with longing. "We planned to get married, but she wanted to wait until I came back."

"Do you think she still waits for you?" Sergeant Ivanov asked, his voice cold.

"I hope so," I said, my voice cracking. "But I don't know."

"And what about Katerina?" Dr. Sokolov pressed. "How do you feel about her?"

"I care about her," I admitted. "But I don't trust my judgment."

The fifth hour was filled with questions designed to sow doubt and suspicion. They asked about my crew, our relationships, and any conflicts we had experienced.

"Vincent, do you trust your crew?" Dr. Sokolov asked.

"Yes," I replied firmly. "We've been through too much together not to trust each other."

"But what if one of them is a traitor?" Sergeant Ivanov suggested. "What if someone has been feeding information to the Germans?"

The suggestion sent a chill through me. "No, that's not possible," I said, trying to maintain my composure.

"Think carefully," Dr. Sokolov urged. "Have you noticed any unusual behavior? Any signs of betrayal?"

I shook my head, feeling a growing sense of unease. "No... I don't think so."

The intensity of the questioning increased in the sixth hour. The interrogators pressed harder, their voices rising, their questions becoming more aggressive.

"Why were you chosen for special attention by Katerina?" Sergeant Ivanov demanded. "What makes you so important?"

"I don't know," I replied, my voice strained. "She said she felt a connection with me."

"And you believed her?" Dr. Sokolov scoffed. "She is a soldier, trained to manipulate and deceive. How can you be sure she wasn't using you?"

The doubt gnawed at me, but I held firm. "I can't be sure. But I want to believe her feelings for me are genuine."

By the seventh hour, I was mentally and physically exhausted. The relentless questioning had taken its toll, and I felt my resolve weakening.

"Vincent, think about your future," Dr. Sokolov said, her voice a mix of sympathy and cold calculation. "Do you want to carry these doubts with you for the rest of your life?"

"No," I whispered, my voice barely audible.

"Then tell us the truth," Sergeant Ivanov pressed. "Who

among your crew can you not trust?"

Tears welled up in my eyes as I struggled to find the words. "I don't know," I cried. "I don't know who to trust anymore."

The final hour was a blur of questions, accusations, and threats. Dr. Sokolov and Sergeant Ivanov pushed harder than ever, their voices blending into a cacophony of confusion and despair.

"Vincent, you must find the traitor," Dr. Sokolov insisted. "Your life, and the lives of your loved ones, depend on it."

"Tell us now, or face the consequences," Sergeant Ivanov threatened.

"I don't know!" I shouted. "I don't know who the traitor is! Quit asking me!"

As the clock struck the end of the eighth hour, the interrogators finally relented. I was left alone in the cold, dark room, my mind a tangled mess of fear, doubt, and exhaustion. When I was finally released and escorted back to my crew, I felt a deep sense of unease, as I'm sure that each of my fellow crewman did. The bond we shared was now tainted by the seeds of doubt planted in our minds. The love and connection I felt for Katerina were now overshadowed by a sense of betrayal.

CHAPTER 27

After the grueling day of interrogation, we were driven back to the house.

The next morning, we gathered in the common room, trying to make sense of everything that had happened. Captain Spansky looked around at each of us, his expression serious.

"Alright, men," he began, his voice steady. "We've been through another round of hell, but we're still here. We need to stay sharp and be ready for anything. If anyone notices anything unusual, speak up. We can't afford any surprises."

Everyone nodded, but there was a noticeable tension in the air. The trust we had once taken for granted now was filled with doubt.

Later that night, as I lay in my bunk, Katerina approached me. Her presence, once comforting, now filled me with a mix of emotions. I was torn between the warmth of her touch and the suspicion that clouded my mind. She sat down beside me, her eyes searching mine.

"Vincent, how are you feeling?" she asked softly.

I hesitated, unsure of how much to reveal. "I'm... managing. It's been rough."

She reached out and took my hand, her touch warm. "I've been worried about you. You've been through so much."

"Why are you so concerned about me, Katerina?" I asked, my voice tinged with suspicion. "Why not anyone else?"

She looked down, her expression pained. "I can't explain it, Vincent. There's something about you, something that draws me closer to you. I care about you."

I wanted to believe her, but the seeds of doubt planted during the interrogations made it difficult.

The next day, we were allowed to spend time outside in the garden. The fresh air was a welcome relief, but unease remained. As we walked, Benny fell into step beside me.

"Vince, something's not right," he said quietly. "Katerina, she's still all over you. Why?"

"I don't know," I admitted. "Katerina says she feels a connection, but it doesn't add up."

"Be careful, Vince. The others are starting to notice, too. They think she's up to something."

I nodded, feeling the weight of his words. "I'll keep my guard up."

That evening, Katerina found me alone in the common room. She sat down beside me, her expression intense.

"Vincent, we need to talk," she said, her voice urgent.

"About what?" I asked, trying to keep my tone neutral.

"About us. About what happens next," Katerina replied, her eyes searching mine.

I sighed, feeling the tension between us. "I don't know, Katerina. Everything is so uncertain. I don't even know if I can trust you," I admitted, my struggle to trust her evident in my tone.

Her eyes filled with tears. "Vincent, please. You have to believe me. I care about you. I want to help you."

"Then tell me the truth," I demanded. "Why are you so focused on me? What are your orders? Are they more than just keeping an eye on me?"

She looked away, her expression conflicted. "I can't... I can't tell you everything. But you have to trust me."

"Trust you?" I scoffed. "How can I trust you when you're keeping secrets?"

She grabbed my hand with a firm grip. "Vincent, I swear, I'm on your side. I want to help you get out of here."

The following days saw more of the same. Katerina's attention never wavered, and it began to multiply my crewmates' suspicion. One afternoon, as we sat in the garden, George approached me again, his expression serious.

"Vince, what's going on with you and Katerina now?" he asked bluntly.

I sighed, running a hand through my hair. "I don't know, George. She says she cares about me, but I don't know what to believe."

"Well, you'd better figure it out quick," George replied. "The others are starting to get more and more suspicious. And honestly, so am I."

That night, as I lay in my bunk, I couldn't shake the feeling that something was wrong. Katerina's words and actions were sincere, but the circumstances were too suspicious. I needed answers.

The following day, I confronted Katerina. "We need to talk," I demanded, my determination and desperation for the truth evident in my voice.

She looked startled but nodded. "Alright, let's go somewhere private."

We found a secluded spot in the garden, away from prying eyes. "Katerina, I need the truth. Why are you so focused on me? Are you just playing games with me?"

She looked down, her expression tormented. "Vincent, I... I was ordered to keep an eye on you, and also to report on everything you said and did, and I mean everything."

My heart sank. "So, it was all a lie? Everything between us?" The weight of her confession crushed me, shattering the fragile trust I had in her.

"No!" she cried, tears streaming down her face. "It wasn't a lie. I do care about you. But I had to follow orders."

"Why me?" I demanded. "Why not Captain Spansky or Lieutenant Lewandowski? Why not the others?"

"I don't know," she admitted. "They never told me why. But you have to believe me, Vincent. My feelings for you are real."

I looked into her eyes, searching for any sign of deceit. "If you care about me, then help me understand. What are they planning?"

She hesitated, then nodded. "Alright. I'll tell you what I know, but you have to promise me something."

"What?" I asked, my voice wary.

"Promise me that you'll trust me. That you'll give us a chance."

I took a deep breath, the weight of her request pressing down on me. "Alright, Katerina. I promise."

Over the next few days, Katerina shared what she knew. The Russians were planning to release us, but they were still suspicious. They believed there might be a traitor among us and wanted to use us to gather more information.

"They're using us as pawns," I muttered, the realization sinking in.

"Yes," Katerina agreed. "But we can use this to our advantage. If we play along, we can gather information of our own. We can find out what else they're after."

"And then what?" I asked. "What happens when they find out we're onto them?"

"We'll deal with that when the time comes," she replied, her expression determined. "For now, we need to trust each other."

Trust. It was a fragile thing, quickly shattered and challenging to rebuild. But as I looked into Katerina's eyes, I saw a glimmer of hope. We could find a way out of this together, or at least I hoped we would.

The last day of our relative comfort brought us a mix of anticipation and dread. We knew our release was imminent, but suspicion remained. Captain Spansky gathered us together for a final meeting.

"Men, we've been through a lot," he began, his voice steady. "But we need to stay focused. Trust is everything. We can't let doubt tear us apart."

Everyone nodded, their expressions solemn. The bond between us remained robust but tested.

As we prepared for whatever lay ahead, I couldn't shake the feeling that our journey was far from over. Katerina's revelations had given me hope but also raised more questions. What were the Russians really after? And what would happen when we finally returned to Italy? Only time will tell. But for now, we had each other. And that was enough.

CHAPTER 28

The following day, the news that we would face another day of interrogation hit us like a bombshell. Dread filled us as they blindfolded and loaded us into the truck once again. The familiar rumble and bumps in the road only heightened our anxiety. As the truck bounced up and down, memories of the previous interrogations flooded my mind. Each jolt felt like a reminder of the relentless questions hurled at me, echoing in the silence of my thoughts. When we arrived, they removed our blindfolds and led us into the same stark building. The sense of déjà vu overwhelmed us as we were separated and taken to different rooms.

"Welcome back, Sergeant Gabrowski," Dr. Sokolov said, her voice eerily calm. "Today will be slightly different."

I nodded, my throat dry. "Different, how?"

"You'll see," she replied, a cryptic smile on her lips.

The questions were designed to confuse and were unlike any I had encountered before.

"Tell me about your last mission," Dr. Sokolov asked.

"We were bombing the synthetic oil fields in Kolin," I replied.

"Are you sure? Didn't you say Ruhland before?"

"No, it was Kolin," I insisted. Doubt crept in as I struggled to maintain my focus.

"Who was with you when you bailed out?" she asked.

"Captain Spansky gave the order," I replied.

"But did he jump first or last?" she pressed.

I hesitated. "He jumped... last, I think."

"You think?" Her eyes bore into mine. "Or do you know?"

"I... don't know," I admitted, feeling a knot of frustration in my chest.

The next phase of the interrogation involved hypnosis again. Dr. Petrov took over, his voice a low, monotonous hum that seemed to seep into my very bones.

"Relax, Vincent. Let your mind drift," he intoned.

As I slipped into the trance, my memories became even more fragmented. Images and sounds overlapped, creating a surreal tapestry of half-remembered events.

"Tell me about Katerina," Dr. Petrov's voice seemed to come from everywhere and nowhere.

"Katerina... she... she cares about me," I murmured.

"And you care about her?" he asked.

"Yes, but... I'm not sure what's real anymore," I confessed.

When I emerged from the hypnosis, the room felt like it was spinning. Dr. Sokolov's questions became more personal and more invasive.

"Vincent, what did Marya say in her last letter?" she asked.

"She... she said she missed me," I replied, trembling.

"Did she say she would wait for you?" Dr. Sokolov's tone was gentle but insistent.

"Yes, but... I don't know if she still is. I don't know if I care," I said, feeling a pang of guilt.

"And what about Katerina? Do you think she will wait for you?" she asked.

"I hope so," I whispered, tears filling my eyes.

The questions shifted to my crew, and I felt the seeds of doubt planted once again.

"Do you trust your crew, Vincent?" Dr. Sokolov asked.

"Yes," I replied, but my voice lacked conviction.

"Are you sure? Think about the interrogations. Has anyone seemed different to you?" she pressed.

"I don't know," I admitted. "Everything's so confusing."

"Perhaps you should be more cautious," she suggested. "Trust is a fragile thing."

By the sixth hour, I was exhausted, both mentally and physically. The relentless questioning and the hypnotic sessions had taken their toll once again.

"Vincent, do you want to go home?" Dr. Sokolov asked, her voice soft.

"More than anything," I replied, my voice reduced to a whisper.

"Then tell us what we need to know," she urged.

"I don't know what you want!" I cried, feeling utterly defeated.

"Just the truth," she said, her eyes cold and calculating.

As the seventh hour dragged on, I felt myself reaching the breaking point. The memories swirled in confusion, and I couldn't distinguish reality from manipulation.

"Vincent, think about Katerina. Think about Marya. Don't you want to protect them?" Dr. Petrov's voice was a haunting echo in my mind.

"Yes, but how?" I asked, my voice breaking.

"By telling us the truth," he insisted. "Who among your crew can you not trust?"

"I don't know!" I shouted, tears streaming down my face. "I don't know who to trust anymore."

The final hour was a blur of questions, accusations, and emotional manipulation. Dr. Sokolov and Dr. Petrov became more demanding than ever, their voices blending into a cacophony of confusion and despair.

"Vincent, you must find the traitor," Dr. Sokolov insisted. "Your life, and the lives of your loved ones, depend on it."

"Tell us now, or face the consequences," Sergeant Ivanov threatened.

"I don't know!" I shouted, "I don't know who the traitor is! I don't know if there is a traitor! Leave me alone!"

The interrogators finally relented as the clock struck the end of the eighth hour. I was left alone in the cold, dark room, my mind a tangled mess of fear, doubt, and exhaustion. When they finally released us and returned us to our original location, we felt overwhelming relief. But the memories of the interrogation were a jumbled mess. We all seemed to have mixed recollections of what had occurred, and it wasn't easy to piece together a coherent narrative. As we gathered in the common room, Captain Spansky addressed us; his voice filled with a mix of relief and caution.

"Men, we're almost out of here," he began. "We've been through hell, but we must stay strong for a little longer. If anyone remembers anything specific about the interrogation, speak up."

There was a murmur of confusion as we all tried to recall the events.

"It was like a dream," Phil said, shaking his head. "I can't remember what was real and what wasn't."

"Same here," Benny added. "It's all a blur."

George nodded. "They did something to our heads. I don't know what, but it messed with our memories."

Captain Spansky looked around the room, his expression serious. "Alright, we'll just have to rely on each other. Stay alert and trust your instincts."

The next morning, we received the news we had been waiting for: we were going home. We would be flying back to Italy aboard a B-17 that would land at an airfield close to our internment location. A sense of relief and excitement filled the room. As we prepared to leave, Katerina approached me, her eyes filled with emotion.

"Vincent, I... I don't know if we'll see each other again."

I took her hand, my heart heavy. "I know. But I believe we will. Somehow, someday."

She smiled through her tears. "Stay safe, Vincent. And remember, I care about you, and I love you."

"I care about you too, Katerina," I replied, feeling a lump in my throat. "I love you. Thank you for everything."

As we boarded the truck to take us to the airfield, I couldn't shake the feeling that our paths would cross again. The bond Katerina and I had formed was too strong to be broken by distance or time.

The flight back to Italy was an interesting experience, highlighted by the Russians shooting at our bomber. As we soared through the skies in the familiar confines of the B-17, the memories of our ordeal seemed to fade into the background. The sense of freedom and the prospect of returning home filled us with renewed hope.

But the mixed memories of the final interrogation lingered. The uncertainty of what happened gnawed at the edges of my mind. I knew that the journey was far from over and that the questions and doubts would follow us long after we landed.

As we touched down at Amendola, the cheers and smiles of our companions greeted us. We were home, but the shadows of our experiences would stay with us. In my heart, I held onto the belief that Katerina and I would be reunited one day.

CHAPTER 29

We returned to Amendola filled with relief, disbelief, and suspicion. We were finally back on friendly soil after surviving the harrowing ordeal of being Russian internees. The base was in a state of transition, with the war in Europe having ended a month earlier. Personnel were preparing for new orders and the eventual return home, yet the heavy tension in the air was undeniable. The sounds of bomber engines and the sight of ground crews maintaining bombers were both familiar and reassuring, reminding us of the battles we had fought. Unlike returning from a mission, where we walked by ourselves, airmen quickly ushered us into debriefings and medical evaluations, each step monitored closely by senior officers, their eyes filled with curiosity and concern.

Then, the same airmen led Captain David Spansky and the rest of the crew to a small conference room where we were to meet with Colonel Harrington. The room was sparse, with a large wooden table and several chairs. The walls were bare, save for a single map of Europe marked with strategic points. The atmosphere was tense, the silence punctuated by the distant hum of activity outside. A few moments later, Colonel Harrington entered, flanked by Major Hastings.

"Gentlemen, welcome back," Colonel Harrington began, his tone formal but warm. "You've been through a lot, and we're here to ensure you're alright and to debrief you on your experiences."

We nodded, our expressions weary but relieved. Harrington

continued, "We'll conduct individual debriefings over the next few days. For now, you're to rest and recuperate."

That evening, the base held a small gathering to celebrate our return. It was an informal event, and a few senior officers, including Colonel Harrington and Major Hastings, attended. The mess hall, transformed for the occasion, had makeshift decorations and a spread of great-smelling food. The atmosphere was light, and we shared stories of our harrowing experiences. The contrast between the lively gathering and the grim memories of our time in captivity was stark. Still, it brought a sense of normalcy that we all craved.

Amidst the gathering, Major Hastings raised a glass of red wine, a local vintage from the vineyards of Foggia. "To the crew of the Hometown Gal," he toasted. "May your bravery and resilience inspire us all." We echoed the toast, our spirits lifted by his words, ready to face whatever challenges lay ahead.

Hastings took a generous sip, savoring the wine's rich flavor. He smiled at us, his eyes shining with admiration and then he collapsed. His glass shattered beside him, a stark reminder of the fragility of life. We stood in disbelief, unable to comprehend what had just happened.

"Medic!" Colonel Harrington shouted, rushing to Hastings' side. White foam oozed out between his lips. We looked on in horror as the base's medical team quickly arrived, but it was too late. Within minutes, Major Hastings was pronounced dead.

The room was in chaos. Officers whispered among themselves, and we now stood in shock. Colonel Harrington took charge, his face grim. "Everyone, remain calm and place your glasses on the table. We'll get to the bottom of this."

The base was quickly locked down, and an investigation was launched. The medical team confirmed that someone had poisoned Hastings, and they traced the source to the glass of wine he had consumed. They found no trace of poison in any of our glasses.

We found ourselves under a cloud of suspicion in spite of the fact that none of us poured the wine. Our recent return from Russian custody, combined with the sudden death of a senior officer, made us prime suspects in the eyes of the investigative team. Tensions rose as we were interrogated once more, this time by our own military, about our time as internees, and what each one of us did prior to Hastings' death.

"We had nothing to do with it," I insisted. "We were celebrating our return. We had no reason to harm Major Hastings. We had no access to the wine."

Colonel Harrington, leading the investigation, became more relentless. "You were Russian internees. You were interrogated. For all we know, you may be compromised."

Colonel Harrington then ordered the crew to be confined to quarters while the investigation continued. The sense of unease grew as rumors spread throughout the base. The base that once felt like a refuge now seemed like a prison.

Two days later, as I sat in my quarters, a knock on the door interrupted my thoughts. I opened it to find a young corporal standing there, his face nervous.

"Sir, this was left for you," the corporal said, handing me an envelope before quickly walking away.

I unfolded the note inside, my heart pounding. It read:

"Trust no one. The truth lies in the vineyard. – A Friend"

I stared at the note, my mind racing. What did it mean? Who had sent it? And how was it connected to Major Hastings' death? I knew I had to find out, but I also knew I had to tread carefully.

I shared the note with Captain Spansky and the rest of the crew. "Someone wants us to investigate the vineyard," I said, my voice low. "We need to find out what's going on."

Spansky nodded, his expression serious. "We'll do it together. We must clear our names and find out who's behind this." Our determination was unwavering, and we were ready to uncover the truth, no matter the cost.

Just as Captain Spansky nodded, another knock at the door interrupted us. Captain Houseman, Major Hasting's replacement, informed us that Colonel Harrington had rescinded the orders confining us, and we were free to spend time in Foggia for some local R&R.

CHAPTER 30

The next day, we fully immersed ourselves in the perilous task of unraveling the truth behind Major Hastings' poisoning. Our investigation had led us to cast suspicion on the vineyard that supplied the wine. Yet, we knew that we needed irrefutable evidence to totally clear our names and unveil the larger conspiracy at play.

Late that evening, Captain David Spansky and I met in a secluded part of the base, away from prying eyes. A chill wind swept through the base, causing me to pull my jacket tighter. Shadows danced around us, turning our secret meeting into a cloak-and-dagger affair.

"We need to find out more about this vineyard," I said, barely above a whisper. "The note mentioned that the truth lies there."

Spansky nodded. "We'll need to be careful. If this is as big as we think, we could be in serious danger."

With a united front, we decided to divide our efforts. I would delve into the base's records, while Spansky would venture to the vineyard under the guise of a casual visitor. We were acutely aware of the need for swift and discreet action.

The following day, I went to the base's records office to see Eddie, who I had befriended when I arrived. Eddie, known for quickly finding the right files and documents, sat at his desk surrounded by paperwork.

"Hey, Eddie, I need a favor," I said whispering, leaning casually against the edge of the desk. "I'm trying to find some information on a vineyard in Foggia. Can you help me out?"

Eddie raised an eyebrow, seemingly hesitant, but nodded. "Sure thing, Vince. Which one?"

"Vigna del Sole Antico."

"Hey, isn't that the vineyard where the wine Major Hastings drank come from? You sure you want to get more involved given your reprieve from Colonel Harrington?"

"Sure is, Eddie. We heard that their wines, less the poison, are the best in Foggia. It's probably the reason why the Luftwaffe leadership confiscated many of their vintages, both to drink while they were here, and to send back to Germany. As for getting more involved, it's what we have to do to clear our names."

I looked for any signs of trouble as Eddie sifted through the records. The hum of the office, the shuffle of papers, and the occasional clink of a typewriter added to the tension. After a while, Eddie returned with a one-inch folder.

"Here you go. This should have everything you need," Eddie said, handing over the folder.

I thanked him, promised to come back with a bottle of wine, and quickly left the office, eager to share the documents.

Meanwhile, Captain Spansky arrived at Vigna del Sol Antico, trying to appear inconspicuous. A friendly old gentleman showed him around the picturesque property.

"Benvenuto to Vigna del Sol Antico," the man said, smiling warmly. "We produce some of the finest wines in the region, and some say, in all of Italy. Would you like to taste some?"

Spansky nodded, accepting a glass of red wine. He took a sip, savoring the rich flavor while keeping his eyes and ears open for any unusual activity. The vineyard was a beautiful expanse of gently rolling hills and lush grapevines, a stark contrast to the grim reality we faced. As the tour continued, he noticed a large, unguarded, building at the far end of the property.

"What's in that building?" Spansky asked casually.

The old man's smile faltered slightly. "Oh, that's just our storage area. Nothing interesting there."

Spansky made a mental note to investigate further and returned to the base, where I was waiting for him. He then told me what occurred.

Back in our quarters, we pored over the documents Eddie had provided. We discovered that the vineyard had recently changed ownership, and the new owner was rumored to have ties to high-ranking German and Russian military officials.

Interestingly, Foggia, and the surrounding region of Puglia have a long history of viticulture and is one of Italy's most important wine-producing regions, known for its extensive vineyards and production of various wine varieties. Despite the hardships and disruptions caused by the War, wine making continued to be an important activity in the region. In Foggia, the residents continued to produce wines, many of which were forcefully taken by the Germans, either for its senior officers or to make ethanol for the fuel-starved German military.

"This is it," I said, pointing to a name on the document. "The new owner is connected to the Russians and privy to notes made during our interrogations as Russian internees. He's also connected to senior officers in both the Luftwaffe and the SS. The previous owner led the group that had been spying on the air crews at Amendola and in particular, us from the moment we landed in Amendola."

Spansky nodded, his expression grim. "Why wouldn't we have shut down the vineyard already? We need to get inside the storage building. I'm sure that where we'll find the answers."

Spansky, a few crew members, and I set out for the vineyard that night. Under the cover of darkness, we approached the building. The air was thick with anticipation, every rustle of leaves or snap of a twig sending our hearts racing. I picked the lock, and we slipped inside. The building was filled with crates of wine, their labels proudly displaying the Vigna del Sol Antico label. But the back room held the real secrets. As we sifted through the documents in the back room, the sound of approaching footsteps froze us in place. "Hide!" I whispered urgently. We barely had time to duck behind a stack of crates before two men entered, their flashlights sweeping the room.

"I heard they're onto us," one man muttered. "We need to move everything out of here tonight."

My heart pounded as we waited for them to leave. When the coast was clear, we resumed our search, finding documents that detailed covert operations, lists of targets, and records of our interrogations. Just as we were about to gather more, the door burst open, and we were face-to-face with the vineyard owner and his armed henchmen.

"Thought you could sneak in and steal wine from me?" the owner snarled, eyes gleaming with malice. "You'll regret this! Prendenteli!"

What followed was a chaotic scramble. We dodged the henchmen's' blows, overturned crates to slow them down, and barely managed to escape through a side window. Running through the vineyard, the alarm sounded behind us, spurring us on. By the time we reached the base, we were breathless but triumphant, clutching the evidence that would bring down the espionage ring. Exhausted and adrenaline-fueled, we burst into Colonel Harrington's office, our breaths ragged, and clothes dirtied from our daring escape. Eddie stood to the side, looking just as anxious as we did since the Colonel's glances at him looked furious.

"Colonel, we have proof," I said, slamming the folder of documents onto his desk. Harrington's eyes narrowed as he began to sift through the pages, the room's tension thickening with each second.

His expression shifted from skepticism to shock. "This is... this is unbelievable," he muttered, more to himself than to us. "You've uncovered a major espionage ring."

He looked up, the weight of the discovery sinking in. "We need to act fast. If they catch wind of this, they'll vanish before we can shut them down."

Harrington's decisiveness was immediate. He hit a button on his desk, summoning his top officers. "Get the base on high alert," he barked as they entered. "Assemble a task force. I want every suspect apprehended by dawn."

As the room exploded into activity, Spansky and I were swept into the whirlwind of the operation. The sense of urgency was noticeable; our every move meticulously planned and executed. We joined the task force, our knowledge of the vineyard's layout crucial for the raid.

Thirty minutes later, under the cover of darkness, we approached Vigna del Sole Antico with military precision. Suffocating tension filled the air, and every touch of our boots to the ground amplified our anxiety. When the signal was given, we moved in, coordinated and silent. Inside, havoc ensued as we stormed the storage building and surrounding areas. Shouts and the sounds of struggle echoed through the night. It was a blur of activity, but our training held firm. One by one, the key figures were apprehended, their operations dismantled piece by piece.

By the time the sun began to rise, we were back at the base. The task force was exhausted but victorious. Colonel Harrington met us as we returned, his stern expression softening.

"Well done," he said, a rare smile tugging at his lips. "You've not only cleared your names but also protected countless lives."

Captain Spansky quickly responded, "Thank you, sir. Thank you also for showing confidence in us by allowing us to be part of the raid."

As we walked out of the Colonel's office, we overheard

him say to Captain Houseman, "Make sure all the additional documents confiscated in the raid are brought to me immediately for my review. I'll store them all in my safe when I am finished."

A profound sense of relief washed over us. Our names were cleared, and the specter of suspicion lifted. As we stood together, watching the base come alive with the new day, we knew that while this chapter was over, our mission was far from complete. The discovery of the espionage ring and the clearing of our names brought immense relief to the Hometown Gal's crew. We had navigated treacherous waters and emerged victorious, but we knew the journey was far from over. United in our resolve to uncover the truth, no matter where it led us, our spirits were buoyed by the sense of accomplishment.

In the days that followed, the base buzzed with activity. The news of the espionage ring's dismantling spread quickly, and the mood shifted from suspicion to admiration. We had proven our loyalty and courage and restored our lost respect.

One day, Captain Spansky and I stood by the airfield, watching the planes come and go.

"Feels good to have our names cleared sir," I said, my eyes fixated on the sky.

Spansky nodded, the weight of the past weeks lifting from his shoulders. "Yeah, it does. But there's still a lot to be done. We need to stay vigilant."

I turned to the Captain, "We will, sir. We've come this far, and we're not backing down now."

As we stood there, united in our resolve, I couldn't help but feel a sense of pride. We had faced incredible odds, uncovered a dangerous espionage ring, and emerged stronger for it. The journey ahead was uncertain, but with my brothers by my side, I knew we could face anything.

The Hometown Gal's crew had been through hell and back,

but our story was far from over. There were still battles to be fought, secrets to uncover, and justice to be served. As we looked to the future, we knew that whatever challenges lay ahead, we would face them together, united and unbreakable.

CHAPTER 31

Stepping off the train in Hamtramck, I felt a rush of emotions—joy, relief, and an undercurrent of sadness. Seeing my family after so long overwhelmed me. Hamtramck's familiar sights and sounds brought a flood of memories, both comforting and bittersweet. Despite the emotional turmoil, I felt relieved to finally be home. As I made my way through the station, I spotted my father standing near the platform, his eyes scanning the crowd. His face lit up when he saw me, and I hurried toward him.

"Dad!" I called out, my voice breaking with emotion.

"Vincent!" he exclaimed, pulling me into a tight embrace. "You're home, son. You're finally home."

We stood there for a moment, just holding each other. When we finally pulled apart, I noticed his eyes' tears matching mine.

"Let's get you home," he said, his voice thick with emotion. "Your sisters can't wait to see you."

The walk to our house was filled with comfortable silence and snippets of conversation about the war, the town, and the family. As we approached the house, I saw my sisters, now teenagers, standing on the porch. They had grown so much since I had last seen them.

"Vincent!" they cried out in unison, rushing toward me.

They engulfed me with hugs, their laughter and tears mingling with mine. We spent the afternoon catching up, sharing stories, and enjoying being together again. The warmth and love in the house were a balm to my soul, soothing the scars left by the war. Later that evening, as we sat around the dinner table, my father looked at me knowingly.

"Son, I know you've been through a lot," he said softly. "And I know there's something you need to tell us."

I nodded, taking a deep breath. "Dad, I met someone during the war. Her name is Katerina. She's special."

My sisters exchanged curious glances, and my father nodded, encouraging me to continue.

"But before I left, there was Marya," I said, trembling. "And I need to talk to her. I owe her that much."

The next day, I arranged to meet Marya at our favorite café. The familiar surroundings brought a wave of nostalgia and a sense of impending sorrow. I couldn't help but feel a knot in my stomach as I waited for her. When she walked in, her face lit up with a smile that quickly faded when she saw the seriousness in my expression.

"Vincent," she said, her voice filled with joy and apprehension. "It's so good to see you."

"Marya," I replied, standing up to hug her. "It's good to see you too. Please, sit down."

We sat across from each other, a heavy silence settling between us. I took a deep breath, trying to find the right words.

"Marya, I need to tell you something," I began. "During the war, I met someone. Her name is Katerina. She was a Russian soldier who guarded the crew after we were shot down. We fell in love."

Marya's eyes widened, and she looked away, blinking back tears. "I see," she said quietly. "And what about us, Vincent? What about everything we talked about?"

"I'm so sorry, Marya," I said, my heart breaking. "I never meant to hurt you. You were my first love, and I'll always cherish that. But things changed. I changed. Katerina and I went through so much together. I couldn't just walk away from that." My voice trembled as I spoke, the weight of my decision heavy on my shoulders.

Marya nodded slowly, her eyes filling with tears. "I understand, Vincent. It's just hard to hear. I always thought we'd have our chance."

"I did, too," I admitted, my voice cracking. "But the War took us in different directions. I hope you can forgive me."

She wiped her eyes and gave me a sad smile. "I do, Vincent. I do forgive you. I want you to be happy."

We talked for a short while longer, reminiscing and sharing each other's hopes for the future. Despite the sadness, there was a sense of closure, and I was grateful for that.

Returning home, I felt a mix of relief and sorrow. I had taken the necessary steps to seek closure with Marya. Though it didn't make it any easier, I felt a sense of resolution. My father and sisters waited for me, their supportive presence reminding me that I was not alone in this journey.

In the days that followed, I settled back into civilian life, surrounded by the love and support of my family. Reconnecting with my father and sisters brought me immense joy. Though the conversation with Marya had been difficult, we both needed to move forward.

As I lay in bed one night, thinking about Katerina, I realized that my journey was far from over. There were still challenges ahead, but I felt a renewed sense of hope and determination. With my family by my side and the hope of a future with Katerina, I knew I could face whatever came next with optimism and anticipation.

CHAPTER 32

Returning to civilian life after the war was a tumultuous journey. Still, the most daunting challenge was the promise I had made to myself: to reunite with Katerina. Our bond, forged during our harrowing captivity, was unbreakable. I couldn't move forward with my life until I had found her and brought her to America. However, given the geopolitical climate and the iron grip of the Soviet government, the task seemed almost insurmountable.

I began by writing letters to various international organizations, hoping to find a way to reach her. Weeks turned into months, and my efforts seemed futile. The Cold War had drawn an iron curtain across Europe, and penetrating it felt nearly impossible.

One evening, while sorting through paperwork at my office, a colleague, John Cooperson, noticed my troubled expression. John was a well-connected man, having served in intelligence during the war. He had a knack for getting things done quietly.

"What's eating at you, Vinny?" he asked, sitting across from me.

I sighed, rubbing my temples. "It's Katerina. I promised her I'd find a way to bring her to the States, but it's like hitting a brick wall at every turn."

John leaned back, a thoughtful expression on his face. "You know, there might be a way. It's not easy, and it might take some time, but I have a few contacts who might be able to help."

John's contacts led me to clandestine meetings with people who had connections within the Soviet Union. These individuals operated in the shadows, navigating the treacherous waters of Cold War politics. Through them, I learned about the bureaucratic hurdles and the delicate negotiations required to bring Katerina to America. One such contact was Dmitri Davanov, a former Soviet diplomat who had defected to the West. Dmitri had a deep understanding of the Soviet bureaucracy and a network of connections that would prove invaluable.

"Vincent," Dmitri said during one of our meetings, "the Soviet government does not easily let go of its citizens, especially those who have had contact with Westerners. But there are ways. It will require patience, resources, and a bit of luck."

I nodded, my determination unwavering. "I'll do whatever it takes. Just tell me what I need to do."

With Dmitri's guidance, I began the arduous process of securing the necessary permissions and documents. The first step was to establish contact with Katerina. Through a series of intermediaries, we sent her a letter explaining my intentions and asking for her agreement to emigrate. Weeks later, a reply came. The letter was from Katerina. My hands trembled as I opened it, my heart pounding with anticipation.

"Dearest Vincent,

I cannot express the joy and hope your letter has given me. The thought of reuniting with you and building a life together is a dream I have held onto since we parted. However, I must warn you that the path will be difficult. The Soviet authorities are not inclined to grant such requests easily. But if you are determined, I am with you every step of the way.

With all my love, Katerina."

Her words filled me with renewed determination. I knew

the road ahead would be fraught with challenges, but I was prepared to face them.

The following steps involved navigating the complex Soviet emigration system. Dmitri helped me draft a formal request to the Soviet government, outlining my intentions and emphasizing the humanitarian aspect of reuniting with a loved one. The request had to pass through numerous bureaucratic layers, each a potential roadblock.

More weeks went by with little progress. Frustration and doubt gnawed at me, but I refused to give up. I made frequent trips to Washington, D.C., meeting with diplomats and officials who could lend their support. John Cooperson's contacts within the State Department proved invaluable, helping to apply diplomatic pressure on the Soviet authorities. During this time, I received sporadic letters from Katerina. Each was a lifeline, reminding me of what I was fighting for. She described her life in Russia, its challenges, and unwavering hope that we would be together again.

One cold winter's day, nearly three months after I started my quest, Dmitri contacted me with unexpected news: "Vincent, there's been a breakthrough. The Soviet authorities are willing to consider your request. Still, they are demanding a substantial payment—a so-called 'administrative fee.' It's essentially a bribe, but it's the only way to expedite the process."

The amount was staggering, far beyond what I could afford. I felt a sinking despair, but John Cooperson stepped in once again.

"Vinny, we'll raise the money," he said firmly. "You have friends here who believe in what you're doing. We'll make it happen."

His words filled me with hope and renewed determination.

We raised the required amount through personal savings, contributions from friends and colleagues, and a discreet fundraising campaign. This was a testament to the strength of our bond formed during the war and the support of those who believed in our cause. With the payment secured, the final steps involved coordinating with the U.S. Embassy in Moscow to facilitate Katerina's departure. The bureaucratic red tape was thick, but the persistent efforts of the embassy staff, combined with the pressure from various diplomats, finally bore fruit. It culminated in months of relentless pursuit, sleepless nights, and the unwavering support of friends and colleagues.

However, the journey to Moscow in late December was not without peril. On more than one occasion, I received anonymous threats warning me to stop my efforts. There were moments when I felt eyes watching me, shadowy figures lurking in the background, reminding me that the stakes were incredibly high.

One night, as I returned to my hotel, a black car followed me at an uncomfortable distance. My heart pounded as I quickened my pace, darting into an alley to lose my pursuer. I pressed myself against the cold brick wall, listening to the car's engine idling at the alley's entrance. After what felt like an eternity, the car drove away, leaving me shaken but more determined than ever. The fear was real, but so was my love for Katerina.

In another instance, I returned to my hotel room and found it ransacked. A chilling note lay on the bed: "Stop now, or you won't live to see her again." I swallowed hard, my resolve wavering but not broken. The danger was real, but so was my commitment to Katerina.

The day I received confirmation of Katerina's approved immigration status made me the happiest man in the world. Her travel arrangements were made, and I anxiously awaited her arrival, which occurred two weeks after my return to the U.S. When I saw Katerina step off the plane at New York Municipal Airport, all the struggles and hardships disappeared. She was as beautiful as I remembered, her gorgeous blue eyes filled with tears of joy and relief. I rushed to her, and we embraced, holding each other tightly as if we would never let go.

"Vincent, we did it," she whispered, her voice choked with emotion. "We're finally together."

"Yes, we did," I replied, my heart overflowing with love and gratitude. "And we're never going to be apart again."

The danger and challenges we faced at that moment seemed like distant memories. We had overcome the impossible, and now we could finally begin our new life together, free from the shadows of the past.

CHAPTER 33

After both our returns from Moscow, we got married. Two days after our marriage, I received an unexpected call. A senior official in the U.S. State Department stated that he and a General Officer from the Department of the Army needed to meet with me. Although disturbing, it made sense, given what it took to get Katerina to the U.S. The following morning, I took a flight and went directly to the agreed-upon meeting location: a small building in Washington, D.C. As I entered an austere conference room, two men greeted me. One was a tall, stern-looking gentleman in a crisp suit. The other wore a decorated military uniform, his presence exuding authority and experience.

"Mr. Gabrowski, thank you for coming on such short notice," the State Department official began, extending his hand. "I'm Richard Standon. This is General Collins."

"Good to meet you," I replied, shaking their hands and sitting down. I assume this has something to do with Katerina?"

Standon nodded. "Indeed. We've been closely monitoring the situation regarding her immigration. While we commend your efforts, it has raised some significant concerns."

General Collins leaned forward, his expression serious. "Vincent, the lengths you went to secure Katerina's freedom have not gone unnoticed, and unfortunately, they have also attracted some unwanted attention. Some members of the Soviet government are not pleased, and there are indications that they may attempt to retaliate."

My heart sank at the thought. "Why would the Soviets do so, given that we did everything correctly? Retaliate? Against whom? Me? Katerina?"

Standon exchanged a glance with Collins before continuing. "Both. The Soviets have a history of making examples from those who defy them. We believe it's imperative to ensure your safety and that of Mrs. Gabrowski."

"But we didn't defy them," I said, pounding my fist on the table. "Are we being watched?" I asked, trying to gather my composure.

"Yes," General Collins said bluntly. "We have reason to believe that Soviet agents may be in the country, keeping tabs on both of you. We need to be proactive in ensuring your protection. It seems that the Soviets found out after they let Katerina go that she knew too much about something that occurred during the War."

"What do you propose?" I asked, trying to keep my voice steady.

Standon leaned back, his fingers steepled. "We're arranging for you and Katerina to be placed under protective surveillance here in D.C. We'll also provide secure housing and constant communication with a security detail."

The room fell silent as I processed their words. The idea of living under surveillance was unsettling. Still, the thought of Soviet agents targeting Katerina and me was even more alarming.

"I understand the necessity," I finally said. "But what about our lives? Our future? How do we build a life with this threat hanging over us?"

General Collins's expression softened slightly. "Vincent, we'll do everything possible to neutralize the threat. In the meantime, our priority is your safety. You've both been through enough. Let us handle this."

Reluctantly, I agreed to the plan. Over the next few days, Katerina and I moved to a secure location, a modest but comfortable house in a quiet neighborhood. The security detail, discreet but ever-present, became a part of our daily lives. Despite the looming threat, we tried to build a semblance of normalcy. Katerina began adjusting to her new life, exploring the neighborhood and making friends. I started working in D.C., albeit under strict security measures. Our lives, though shadowed by danger, began to take shape.

One evening, as Katerina and I sat on the porch, watching the sunset, she turned to me, her eyes reflecting the fading light. "Vincent, do you ever regret bringing me here? All this trouble because of me..."

I took her hand, squeezing it gently. "Never. You're worth every risk and every challenge. We're in this together and will face whatever comes our way."

She smiled, her eyes filled with gratitude and love. "I don't know what I'd do without you. You've given me a new life."

"And you've given me a reason to fight," I replied, pulling her close. "We'll get through this, Katerina. I promise."

As the days turned into weeks, the initial tension began to ease. We adapted to our new reality, finding strength in each other. But the threat was never far from our minds, a constant reminder of our sacrifices and the enemies we had left behind. One night, as we lay in bed, the phone rang. I answered it, my heart pounding. It was Standon.

"Vincent, we have news. Our agents have identified and detained several Soviet operatives in the area. We neutralized the immediate threat, but we'll continue to protect both of you just to be on safe side."

Relief washed over me, and I thanked him before hanging up. Turning to Katerina, I shared the news, and she hugged me tightly, tears of relief streaming down her face. For the first time in months, I felt a glimmer of hope. The road ahead was still uncertain, but with the immediate danger behind us, we could finally envision a future free from fear.

As we drifted off to sleep, I held Katerina close, silently vowing to protect her and build the life we had fought so hard to achieve. Together, we faced unimaginable challenges and emerged stronger.

CHAPTER 34

Just when we thought our lives were back to normal, there was a knock at our door. The unexpected sound made Katerina and I exchange worried glances. I opened the door to find Richard Standon and General Collins standing there, their expressions serious but not unfriendly.

"Mr. Gabrowski," Standon began, his tone formal. "May we come in?"

"Of course," I replied, stepping aside to let them in.

As they entered our modest living room, Standon and General Collins exchanged glances before taking seats on the couch. Katerina and I sat across from them.

"We have some important news," Standon began. "Vincent, you've been given a special assignment that requires both of you to relocate."

"Relocate?" I repeated, feeling a mix of curiosity and apprehension. "To where? Why?"

General Collins leaned forward, his voice steady and authoritative. "To the city of Healdsburg in Northern California. The assignment is sensitive, and we believe it's in the best interest of national security and your safety."

Katerina's eyes widened in surprise. "But why Healdsburg? What's the assignment about?"

Standon smiled, though it was a smile tinged with gravity. "Healdsburg is an ideal location due to its relative remoteness and the specific nature of the assignment. Vincent, your skills and experiences have made you a prime candidate for this mission. It involves both intelligence work and leveraging your military background."

I looked at Katerina, who nodded slightly, signaling her support. Turning back to the officials, I asked, "What exactly will I be doing?"

Collins handed me a sealed envelope. "This contains all the details you need to know. You are to read it privately and destroy it afterward. The assignment is crucial, Vincent, and we need you to be fully committed."

I took the envelope, feeling its significance. "And what about Katerina? What does this mean for her?"

Standon's expression softened. "Katerina will be safe in Healdsburg. We will provide you with secure housing and ensure you are well-protected. Her presence is essential to maintaining the cover story for your assignment."

Katerina reached out and took my hand. "We'll do it, Vincent. Whatever it takes, we'll do it together."

I squeezed her hand, feeling a surge of gratitude and resolve. "Alright. We'll go to Healdsburg."

Collins stood up, extending his hand. "Thank you, Vincent. Your country appreciates your service. You'll both leave within the week. Arrangements are being made as we speak."

As Standon and Collins left, Katerina and I sat silently, processing the sudden turn of events. Finally, I opened the envelope and read through the contents, feeling the enormity of the task ahead.

"We're doing this," I said softly, looking at Katerina.

She smiled, a determined glint in her eyes. "Yes, we are. And we'll face whatever comes our way, just like we always have."

The following days were filled with preparations. We packed

up our belongings, said our goodbyes to the few friends we had made, and got ready for our move to Healdsburg. The sense of impending change was both daunting and exhilarating. When the day of our departure arrived, we excitedly boarded the plane with a tinge of trepidation. As the aircraft soared into the sky, I glanced at Katerina, who smiled reassuringly.

Healdsburg awaited us, a new chapter filled with uncertainty and promise. Together, we were ready to face whatever challenges lay ahead, united by our love and our shared determination to build a future free from fear and filled with hope.

CHAPTER 35

We finally settled into our new home and surroundings in the Russian River Valley. The tranquility of the area, with its gently rolling hills dotted with vineyards and framed by towering redwoods, offered a sense of peace we had longed for. It seemed like the perfect place to rebuild our lives.

One crisp winter early afternoon, as the golden sunlight filtered through the Valley, I walked to our mailbox. I found a letter that would change our lives—and the lives of the crew of Hometown Gal—forever. The envelope was plain, with no return address, and its non-descriptive appearance hinted at its gravity. Curious and apprehensive, I opened the envelope and began reading. As my eyes scanned the words, my mind went into a whirlwind of thought—the same whirlwind I later found out every crew member felt when they read their letters.

"Vincent,

It has been six months since our days in Foggia, and I hope this letter finds you well. I have something urgent to discuss with you and the rest of the crew. Enclosed are coordinates to a safe location where we can meet in person. This matter is of the utmost importance.

Yours sincerely, Colonel Harrington."

My heart pounded as I absorbed the contents of the letter. Memories of the War, the missions, and the bond we shared as a crew flooded back with overwhelming force. What could necessitate such a sudden and urgent call to action?

Sensing my distress, Katerina came up behind me and gently placed a hand on my shoulder. "Vincent, what's wrong? What does the letter say?" Her concern was evident in her voice, her eyes filled with worry.

I handed it to her, watching her eyes widen with each passing sentence. "Do you think it's safe? Do you think it's a trap?" she asked, her voice tinged with concern.

"I don't know," I admitted, feeling a knot of anxiety tighten in my chest. "But it sounds serious. I need to call the crew."

Within hours, I reached each member of the Hometown Gal crew. Their reactions mirrored my shock, confusion, and a growing sense of duty. Each of us had started building new lives, but the bonds forged in the crucible of war could not be ignored.

"Vince, do you think this is legit?" Benny's voice crackled over the phone, the unease evident.

"I can't say for sure," I replied. "But we owe it to ourselves and each other to find out. If there's a chance we can help, we need to take it."

We all agreed to meet at the designated location, a secluded cabin deep in the Sierra Nevada. The secrecy surrounding our orders was thick, adding to the tension and suspense. Still, there was also an undeniable sense of purpose that united us.

I couldn't shake the feeling that something was off as we arrived at the cabin. The familiarity of Colonel Harrington's handwriting clashed with the strange and urgent nature of the message, creating a sense of suspense and anticipation. As the last of us entered the cabin, a gentleman stepped forward to greet us, but it wasn't Colonel Harrington.

"Gentlemen, it's good to see you all," he began, his formal tone edged with something I couldn't quite place. "We have a lot to discuss, and time is of the essence."

He handed out letters to each of us, meticulously marked with our names and stated, "Before we begin, I need you all to read these silently to yourselves."

We opened the letters and began to read, and as I scanned the words, a strange feeling washed over me. It was as if a switch had been flipped in my mind, triggering memories and emotions that didn't seem to belong to me. Glancing around the room, I saw similar expressions on the faces of my comrades—confusion, realization, and an eerie sense of déjà vu.

"What's going on?" Benny asked, his voice shaking. "Why do I feel like I know something I shouldn't?"

And then, as if a switch had been flipped, the room seemed to go dark, plunging us into a disorienting blackness that seemed to swallow us whole!

CHAPTER 36

For me, 56 years later, the switch was flipped again, only this time there was light! In 2002, while working around the workshop, I fell and hit my head, temporarily knocking me out. Five minutes later, I awoke thinking that I could be concussed. However, suddenly, the memories of 1945 came rushing back. I realized that the Russian psychologists had programmed the crew of the Hometown Gal during our internment.

The implications were staggering. We had been unknowingly manipulated; our minds turned into weapons against our own country. As the weight of the situation settled over me, I realized the actual danger the United States and the world faced. I assumed the other crew members had yet to become deprogrammed like me. I could tell no one, not even Blondie. However, I was determined to dedicate my life to counteracting what had been in place for many years.

I faced the battle alone at the start, but I knew I would ferret out the right people to support the most incredible mission of my life. The challenge I faced would take years to overcome, and now it's left to you, Michael, to finish the war.

After my revelation, I meticulously documented every resurfacing memory, and researched techniques to protect my mind from potential triggers. Trusting no one, I finally reached out to Dr. Jonathan Miles, a renowned psychologist, given his experience in psychological warfare and deprogramming techniques.

Meeting him in a secluded location, I cautiously shared my story. "Dr. Miles, I need your help. I believe my crew and I were subjected to intense psychological programming by the Russians during the war. I've been deprogrammed, but I must know how to protect myself and help my crew."

Dr. Miles listened intently, his expression grave. "Vincent, what you're describing is highly complex. Deprogramming isn't a simple process, and you've managed to break free, which is remarkable. We need to approach this systematically. First, we need to understand the programming's triggers and extent."

For months, Dr. Miles and I worked together in secret. He taught me mental techniques to shield my thoughts. He helped me develop strategies to subtly test the crew's programming without alerting them. We devised a plan to identify and neutralize potential triggers embedded in our psyche.

As time passed, I carefully reconnected with each crew member under the guise of rekindling old friendships. Each interaction was a test, a subtle probe into their mental state. I was concerned to find that all had been triggered. It was a delicate balance, trying to awaken their true selves without activating any hidden commands that would derail my mission. I devised a strategy to gradually introduce them to the truth, planting seeds of doubt and allowing them to realize that they had been programmed during our interrogations as internees.

One evening, while visiting Benny, I decided to test the waters. "Benny, do you ever think about our time after we were shot down? I've had these strange memories, almost like dreams, but they feel real."

Benny's eyes flickered with a brief, unreadable emotion before he shrugged. "Sometimes, Vince. But I try not to dwell on it. What's the point?"

I nodded, gauging his reaction. "Yeah, you're right. I just thought I'd ask. It's been on my mind a lot lately."

The conversation left me more determined. Benny's response suggested he was still under the influence, but the seed of doubt had been planted. Over the following weeks, I introduced similar conversations with other crew members, each pushing further and further into breaking the bonds that the programming glued into their minds.

As I worked to unravel the programming, I also sought allies within the intelligence community. Through Dr. Miles' connections, I met Agent Sarah Sisson, an operative specializing in counterintelligence. She became invaluable, providing insights and resources to aid my mission. Our meetings, filled with intense discussions and planning sessions, brought us closer to our goal.

"Vincent," Sarah said during our covert meetings, "We need to be cautious. If the Russians catch wind of what we're doing, they'll stop at nothing to silence us. But I believe we can do this. Your knowledge combined with our resources gives us a fighting chance."

Together, we developed a comprehensive plan to deprogram the crew, one by one, and dismantle the Russian network responsible for the programming. We identified safe houses, secured communication channels, and established emergency protocols. To ensure our success, we meticulously planned every detail.

The final phase involved gathering each crew member separately in a secure location where Dr. Miles and Agent Sisson would assist me with the deprogramming. It was a risky move, but we had no other choice.

"Are you sure they'll come?" Agent Sisson asked, her eyes scanning the empty room.

"They'll come," I replied, my voice steady. "We've been through too much together for them to ignore this."

With Dr. Miles' guidance, we initiated the deprogramming

process. It was a grueling journey, filled with moments of despair and breakthroughs. But I was determined, and one by one, my brothers began to reclaim their minds, their true selves emerging from the fog of manipulation.

Tom was the first to arrive. "Vince, what's all this about?" he asked suspiciously.

"It's complicated, Tom. But trust me, we're here to help you," I said, leading him to a chair. "Just sit tight and listen to Dr. Miles."

As the session progressed, Tom's expression shifted from confusion to a dawning realization. "I remember now... the things they did to us."

"We're going to help you through this, Tom," Dr. Miles assured him.

Throughout the process, Dr. Miles and Agent Sisson worked tirelessly, their expertise evident as they dismantled the psychological barriers the Russians had implanted. Each session was a battle, but we began to see progress.

"Vince, I feel like I've been in a fog for years," Benny admitted during his session, tears welling in his eyes.

"Thank you for bringing us back."

"We'll get through this together," I reassured him, gripping his shoulder.

Dr. Miles and Agent Sisson agreed that in the final sessions, I would be alone in the room to hear what each crew member was programmed to do. The revelations were shocking, each a piece of a giant puzzle.

"Vince," Dr. Miles said, his voice grave. "Be prepared for anything. The things they've been programmed to do are beyond comprehension."

"I know," I replied, readying myself for what would come. "But I have to see this through. I have to undo what has been done."

As each man faced his deepest fears and darkest memories, I realized the enormity of our task. But with every breakthrough, hope replaced the despair that had gripped us for so long.

Eventually, armed with the secrets of each crew member, my mission shifted to connecting the dots and doing whatever was necessary to protect the U.S. and the world. Unfortunately, my luck ran out. Knowing too much has jeopardized my life, and the end draws nearer with each passing day. Anticipating this outcome, I carefully constructed a plan for you, Michael, to carry out with my guidance and the help of a select few I trust implicitly. This small band of dedicated individuals pledged their support to you. Pay close attention to the clues I've left behind and always remember that *'and then there was ONE!'* doesn't mean me. It means you!

CHAPTER 37

As he stood by their graves, one could see a warm, golden glow over the rolling hills. The rich scent of earth and blooming flowers mingled in the air. The quiet rustle of leaves and the distant hum of life in the town below starkly contrasted with the grief that weighed heavily on Mickey's heart.

As the last mourners departed, Mickey remained, lost in thought. The tranquility of Healdsburg, with its peaceful hills and quiet town, seemed almost ironic, a stark contrast to the turmoil in Mickey's mind. It was a place that promised peace, yet his mind churned with memories of his father and mother and the weight of his unfinished business: solving their murders.

A soft voice interrupted his reverie. "Michael, are you alright?" It was Sarah Sisson, one of the trusted individuals Gunner had tapped to ensure Mickey would succeed with what Gunner had started. Her presence signified that, in the future, Mickey's mission would not be faced alone.

Mickey nodded slowly, turning to face her. "It's just... it's a lot to take in. As he said this, he didn't recognize her. "Who are you?"

Sarah stepped back and offered a faint smirk, her eyes focused intently. "My name is Sarah Sisson. I worked with your father over the years but never had a chance to meet either you or your mother."

They stood in silence for a moment. Finally, Sarah spoke again, her tone resolute. "Your father told me to tell you the world will be grateful for what you will accomplish."

Perplexed, Mickey's voice was firm as he stated, "I have only one job to accomplish, and that is to find out who murdered them. Nothing else matters!"

His determination echoed in the quiet cemetery, a testament to his unwavering resolve.

With that, Mickey walked slowly and turned away from the graves, while Sarah smiled and hummed an unknown melody quietly.

Dear Reader,

Thank you for reading *Hometown Gal*, the first prequel novel in the *Wine Flights of Murder* series.

Hometown Gal is published by Skalmystoricpoe, LLC, a small independent publisher.

Please consider leaving a review or rating at the site of your purchase. Reviews help us to reach a greater audience and are always appreciated.

The *Wine Flights of Murder* series also includes the already published, *Russian Red*. In 2025, another prequel and a sequel are expected to be published.

Other books published by Skalmystoricpoe, LLC, include *Best Friends, Best Forgotten* and *Best Friends, Best Forgiven*, the first two novels in the *Best Friends, Best Forgotten* series.

Visit **wineflightsofmurder.com** for the latest information on the *Wine Flights of Murder* series.

See the Proof-of-Concept Movie Trailer for *Best Friends, Best Forgotten* and learn how you can help make the full-length feature film a reality at **BFBFMovie.com**.

ABOUT THE AUTHOR

Paul Skalny

Paul Skalny grew up in Detroit and currently resides in Southeast Michigan.

Paul's love for wine equals only his passion for writing. For over a decade, Paul, an economist and engineer by education and trade, has written thousands of inspirational poems.

The Wine Flights of Murder series is inspired by his father, John, a World War II veteran who served in the U.S. Army Air Corps. Besides writing, Paul continues to be actively engaged in technologies that will make a difference in people's lives.

Made in the USA
Monee, IL
23 August 2024